OIL-FREE

By

Wilbur Shapiro

Dedication

In a global economy, innovation is what keeps America on top. This book is dedicated to the innovators of America, especially to those innovators whose inventions or discoveries have benefitted mankind.

D1166299

1

SUMMARY

Wilson Shindler's dream was to develop an Oil-Free piston engine. Besides difficult technical hurdles, he had to overcome significant headwinds of corporate greed and evil. Ultimate success leads to a decision fork that would have a profound effect on his future way of life.

GERM

Wilson Shindler kissed his wife Maureen on the cheek and headed out the door for his drive to work. Today was somewhat special because he was to present to management a research program requiring company funding. Wilson was a mechanical engineer with a Master's degree and has had 10 years' experience in the private sector. He was involved in the technology of Tribology, which encompasses lubrication and friction and wear. His specialty was fluid film bearings including both journal and thrust bearings with a liquid or gaseous lubricant. A journal bearing has a circular shape that surrounds the rotating shaft and resists radial loading. A thrust bearing resists loads in an axial direction against a rotating collar attached to the shaft. Today Wilson was to pitch a germ of an idea to management in the hope that internal development money would be available to develop his idea.

He arrived at Mechanical Analytics, Inc. early so that he could set-up his power point presentation, which was scheduled for 9:00 AM before the Internal Resource Committee. The committee consisted of the president of the company Hansel Agrarian, several group managers and the company lawyer who was available for patent purposes. Wilson had 30 minutes to make his presentation as there were

3 other promotions on the meeting docket. He presented his case as follows:

"The ultimate objective is to produce an Oil-Free piston engine. This may be accomplished by using pressurized air to replace the oil lubricant. Air bearing technology will be prevalent. Initial concentration will be on the piston itself, which is presently lubricated by splash lubrication. The idea I am presenting utilizes the gas that is compressed by the piston to produce a low clearance, but high stiffness gas film between the piston and the surrounding walls. The gas film will prevent contact between the piston and the walls and the friction will be significantly reduced. The leakage will be very small and the overall effect will be higher efficiency.

Some six to ten percent of power in reciprocating Internal Combustion (IC) engines is lost through friction of mechanical components. A major contributor is piston friction due to rings and viscous shearing of splash oil along the piston skirt. Piston friction contributes over 33% of losses, if the pumping load is included. On a purely mechanical basis, piston friction contributes well over 90% of the mechanical losses. By lubricating the piston with pressurized gas, produced by normal operation of the engine, a significant reduction in piston friction can be accomplished. Piston skirt shearing forces are proportional to the viscosity of the fluid being sheared. The viscosity of air is approximately 1/1000 of oil so that a commensurate reduction in friction can be theorized. The net result of successful gas lubricated piston technology is reduced fuel consumption and reduced dependence on foreign oil. An additional advantage of a gas lubricated piston is ability to operate at high temperatures without oil degradation, which is important particularly to the development of adiabatic diesel engines. High temperature operation itself translates to improved efficiency. There are approximately 65 million automobile type vehicles produced annually. This translates to at least 260 million pistons. The economics are astounding. On a mass production basis the annual value approaches at least six or seven billion dollars

The following slides show some conceptual ideas for piston configurations. In addition to the piston itself there are other components requiring lubrication including the crankshaft bearings, the connecting rod bearings and the piston wrist pins. Each of these components will be shown on the accompanying slides. To accomplish lubrication of these components will require an external source of air pressure. I have been thinking of employing a Resonant Piston Compressor (RPC) that our company is developing. The RPC does not require oil, and uses magnetic bearings. Operation of the RPC in a resonant mode significantly reduces the amount of energy necessary to drive it. The crank shaft bearings will be hydrodynamic air bearings with a pressurized inlet to increase load capacity. The wrist pins will be fed with air pressure and avoid contact by squeeze film lubrication. The connecting rod bearings will operate via a combination of hydrodynamics and squeeze film and again will be lubricated with air.

To start this research, I am proposing that we concentrate on piston lubrication. I would like to do analytical studies of the concepts presented, complete designs and then build a test rig to confirm designs. To initiate the process, I am proposing a one year program with internal funding of $250,000."

Wilson was sure the committee was awed by his presentation and recognized the potential for a major business activity. They congratulated him on his presentation and indicated that a decision would be available in several weeks.

LOCAL REJECTION

That evening Wilson discussed the presentation with Maureen. "I had a very interesting day today. I presented to management a germ of an idea for an Oil-Free piston engine in the hopes of obtaining some internal funding to pursue the concept. If the idea ever comes to fruition it could mean billions for the company and some pretty healthy rewards for me. I am expecting a response in several weeks." Maureen replied "Wilson, I know you are very creative and have a great imagination. I am sure you know that I wish you the very best, and I love you dearly." Wilson smiled and said "My dear I wish you were on the selection team."

In the following days Wilson returned to his normal routine. Mechanical Analytics is a Research and Development Organization. It was formed by two former employees of The Major Electric Company, Hansel Agrarian and Dr. Bruno Stickler. The organization mostly does contract research with both industry and government. Hansel is a respected business man and performs most of the business functions of the organization. Bruno, on the other hand is the technical guru of the company and is also heavily involved in marketing. The company has accumulated an excellent staff of advanced degree scientists and engineers. Most of the staff is very busy satisfying customer demands and bringing in a reasonable profit to the organization. Unfortunately, most of the original ideas generated by the organization become the property of the sponsoring company who then can assume exclusive rights to patents and the concepts created. Hansel recognizes that there are limitations to the growth of an R&D organization and is driven to find a product base that could result in mass production and extensive profits. However, a successful product must be launched and created by internal funding at the exclusion of other organizations. Wilson had high hopes that his idea for an Oil-Free piston engine would be a product that Mechanical Analytics would be interested in. It would be difficult for the company to embark on an entire engine manufacturing effort, but the concepts could produce patents and licensing agreements could be made with prospective producers, generating royalty income. Also, certain components of the engine, such as Resonant Piston Compressors could be a successful and profitable product that could be manufactured by Mechanical Analytics. Wilson hoped that management would see things the same way he did.

Some two weeks later, Wilson received an internal memo that read as follows:

INTERNAL MEMO

From: Internal R&D Committee

To: Wilson Shindler

We regret to inform you that your request for internal funding for the development of an Oil-Free piston engine is denied. The committee congratulates you on an excellent presentation and a very worthwhile idea. Unfortunately, at the present time, internal resources are very limited and all internal R&D programs are on hold.

We encourage you to seek outside development funding as we believe that a program as you described would bring significant and needed income to the company.

Wilson did not know how to interpret this memo. The request denial was not the question, but the statement regarding resources and the suggestion that he seek external funding was baffling. It seemed that all technical personnel were very busy and were bringing in project funds. Also, the suggestion that Wilson solicit outside funding was puzzling. Before he could market for outside funding some preliminary effort would be required. Would Mechanical Analytics pay for preliminary analysis and proposal preparation? There was no mention of support for that activity in the memo.

Furthermore, any outside contractor who provided support would want exclusive rights to whatever is developed. Why should the company give that away? It was becoming clear to Wilson, that the company expected him to donate his own time to the development of an outside program. The more Wilson thought about it, the more incensed he became. He decided to forget the whole thing and concentrate on the contracts he was responsible for. Some of the questions that entered Wilson's mind would be answered in a matter of days, due to events that would not be precipitated by him.

That evening Wilson discussed the memo with Maureen. She quickly grasped the situation and declared "Wilson, it sounds like Mechanical Analytics is in financial trouble. Perhaps we should consider a Plan B. I have a pretty healthy teaching career at the local elementary school, and we cannot give up the benefits that I have been able to accrue. Therefore, we cannot leave the area." Wilson replied, "Maureen, don't get over dramatic. I am sure Mechanical Analytics will survive. I like my job and I have built up a good client base. I intend to forget about the rejection and continue serving clients as before." Maureen commented "OK Wilson, we shall see."

BANKRUPTCY

Several days later the bombshell erupted. Hansel Agrarian called a meeting with the entire staff to be held in the model shop area at 2:00PM. A portable microphone and speakers were set up. Some 450 staff of Mechanical Analytics were standing and waiting for Hansel's remarks. Hansel entered and began his speech. *"I will come directly to the point. Our company is in deep financial debt and we have declared bankruptcy. Most of the problems had to do with bad investments that the company made. For example, the New Jersey company Joliet Manufacturing who make components for the DOD has been accused of falsifying inspection records and was assessed a significant fine and must re-inspect already delivered material. There have been other investments that went sour. The creditors have agreed that we must complete projects that are in progress. Portions of the company will be sold to other interested parties. That means that some of you will be working for another organization. Unfortunately, other personnel will be dismissed and layoff notices will be delivered shortly. I always thought that our company had a bright future and I am sorry that it must end like this. Further instructions will be forthcoming from the managerial staff."*

Wilson was in a state of shock. He could not believe what he had just heard. He felt as if a two ton anvil had been dropped on his shoulders. He felt weak to his stomach and hoped he would not retreat to the men's room to throw up. He had diligently worked for Mechanical Analytics for over ten years and had developed an excellent rapport with customers and the support staff. Wilson anticipated a long career with the organization until it was time to retire. Now, alternative options were thrust upon him. After the meeting, there was considerable chatter among the staff. It was rumored that Hansel Agrarian and Bruno Stickler had been at odds for some time as to what direction the company should go. Hansel was anxious and wanted immediate returns, thus the acquisition format. Bruno wanted to build from within, which was the logical and more productive way to expand the organization. Wilson was unaware of the friction between the two founders and owners of the company, but as he thought about the situation, the reason for failure of the organization became clearer. When Hansel and Bruno were on the same page, the company thrived. When they took opposite tacks, problems became inevitable. As far as Wilson was concerned, some heavy thinking on what to do next was required. What was his Plan B to be?

That evening he discussed the situation with Maureen. "You were right about the company having financial problems. With my concentration on my work, I was oblivious to what was going on around me. Mr. Agrarian threw away a promising organization in his rush to mass produce something. He was ill advised to go the route that he did". Maureen replied, "So where does that leave us. I prefer not to move elsewhere since I have my tenure in the school system and I enjoy my job very much". Wilson commented, "I have been thinking all afternoon. I might be with the group to be sold, but I do not know what that entails with respect to location, salary and benefits. I believe the best course of action for me is to go into private consulting. We can make an office out of the fourth bedroom. I can upgrade my computer to work station status, buy an all in one laser printer and I could be in business. I have developed quite a few computer codes that will be indispensable and I have formulated concepts for additional codes. My reputation with industry and government is very good. Furthermore, I would be eligible for Small Business Innovative Research Contracts (SBIR's) that could provide substantial funding. After dinner I will go upstairs and formulate a plan of action".

The plan Wilson came up with included the following:

- Submit a letter of resignation to Mechanical Analytics to be affected immediately. Wilson will offer to complete his present project load on a consulting basis. His consulting fees will be based on his present salary plus benefits.

- Purchase a computer upgrade to workstation status that will have capabilities to handle large technical computer codes. The codes he envisions are those that he alone has generated or will generate. He intends to take the necessary steps to upgrade the codes and make them user friendly. The codes will not only permit Wilson to accomplish advanced work, but they could also become a sale item.

- Visit a lawyer to establish a corporation. He has selected the name Tribos Engineering as the name of his company. Tribos means rubbing surfaces in Greek and forms the basis for the name Tribology, which is the science of friction and wear.

- Set up a working office in the fourth bedroom

- Solicit Homer Jennings, an expert design engineer, who recently retired from Mechanical Analytics, to work with Wilson on a contract basis.

- Generate Marketing literature and transmit to relevant companies who might use the services of Tribos Engineering.
- Determine how to handle health and retirement benefits.

When Wilson wrote all this down, it indicated a significant amount of work to do and he presumed that for a while he would be working very hard and putting in many long hours. Even though a mountain was ahead of him it was somehow, refreshing to Wilson that he would be master of his own destiny.

The next day, Wilson submitted a letter of resignation:

Memo

To: Human Resources

From: Wilson Shindler

I hereby resign from Mechanical Analytics (MA) effective immediately. I can complete my present project work load as a consultant to the company. I am solely involved in two major projects, a buffer seal with NASA and a gas bearing rotary spindle for Jason Manufacturing. The technical details for both programs have been completed and they require final reports. The NASA program can be completed in two months at an estimated cost of $27,000. The Jason Manufacturing *report can be completed in an additional 3 weeks at an estimated cost of $12,000. If these terms are agreeable then please authorize purchase orders to me. If MA wishes other personnel to complete these programs, I will provide one week's assistance at a cost of $4000 for transition purposes.*

He was sure that the memo put MA in a difficult position. Since he had been solely involved in both programs, a change of personnel would not be looked upon favorably by either client. Although, the news of the bankruptcy was promulgated locally, it was not yet public knowledge. Wilson was gathering his personal belongings from his office when he received a call from Jim Clairborne, his immediate supervisor. "Wilson, could you come over to my office for a chat."

Wilson sat down in front of Jim's desk as Jim commented, "Don't you think your resignation is premature. Why don't you wait and see what happens next? You would probably be with a group that was being sold to another organization. Perhaps that would be a good move for you." Wilson replied, "When Hansel gave his speech to the staff, I was blindsided. I have given ten years of hard effort to this organization only to be rewarded with bankruptcy. I had great hopes for Mechanical Analytics and my position with the company. I was dedicated to retiring here. What grabs me is that the staff is very busy producing excellent technology for our clients and they are very happy with us. Then, I come to find out that Hansel Agrarian was gambling away our future. I bet he comes out of this bankruptcy richer, while the rest of us struggle for what to do next. I have nothing but a bitter taste in my mouth and I feel deceived. I want out and nothing will change my mind. Jim, you don't even know where you are going to end up." Sensing Wilson's frustration, Jim condescended and said "OK Wilson, we will let you know about a consulting contract and best of luck." Wilson replied "Same to you."

That afternoon Wilson went to see his lawyer who had taken care of his will and other matters related to death and incapacity due to old age. After discussing Wilson's consulting objectives the formation of an S corporation was decided. Wilson, at this time, wanted to be a lone operator. If outside help would be required he would do so on a contract basis. The S Corporation would allow business expenses and profits to be taxed on the personal income tax basis. This allows S corporations to avoid double taxation on the corporate income. The lawyer said that he would have Tribos Engineering set up as an S corporation in several weeks.

There were quite a few open items on Wilson's checklist. The next order of business was to procure his tools of the trade, namely a workstation computer with the latest Intel chips, large memory and large drive capacity. He studied the options on the internet and decided on a mobile workstation, which was essentially a souped up lap top. He selected a lap top because he could use it to work at home and travel with it for presentations and to work at a client's facility. He made his choice and ordered the computer over the internet. He also ordered a laser printer and other paraphernalia necessary for a working environment. Wilson went to an Office Products store to order a desk and printer stand. He also ordered some book cases and filing cabinets. Wilson was learning that it was not so cheap to get ready for business.

When Wilson returned home he called Homer Jennings. Homer had worked closely with Wilson at Mechanical Analytics, and he retired several weeks ago. Homer was surprised at the bankruptcy and he asked Wilson, "What do you plan to do?" Wilson replied, "I resigned from MA and am making preparations to go into private consulting. I would like to use you for design purposes on a contract basis. How do you feel about that?" Homer replied "I would be pleased to help however I can. I prefer to do initial layout work on my board in the basement, but detailing should be done by someone else. Edgar Neuman does lots of detail work and he purchased a drafting plotter to ensure professional results. If you would like, I can contact him and advise him of your plans. I am sure he would be willing to contribute." Wilson responded, "That sounds great Homer. It will take some time for me to get started, but I will be in touch."

Wilson had a 401K retirement account at Mechanical Analytics and he presumed that it was safe from the company creditors. However, as soon as possible he intended to convert the account to a personal IRA. Wilson wanted to rid himself of any ties to his old company. He intended to discuss the situation with the MA human resources department the next day. He also wanted to find out about the company life insurance policy, to which he made monthly contributions. He presumed that he could continue the policy on a personal basis.

A primary activity for Wilson's startup company was to promulgate his expertise to private and government institutions who might utilize his services. He initiated preparation of a Curriculum Vita which outlined his capabilities, and past experience and also he initiated preparation of a list of his publications and patents. The preparation also included a forwarding letter stating the objectives of his new company. In addition he began making a list of contacts that might be interested in his services. The list included his previous and present companies that he had worked for, plus many others that he hadn't worked for but who might be interested in his services. He estimated that effort would take at least one month of his time.

The following day Wilson received a telephone call from Jim Clairborne. "Wilson, I have good news. Your proposal to complete your existing programs has been approved. Purchase orders will be cut and sent out today. You will be allowed on the premises and can use the necessary equipment to complete the projects." Wilson replied "That's good news Jim. The funds are welcome and will provide some foundation as I attempt to get established. I have already spent several thousand on what I anticipate I will need to get going." Jim continued, "Incidentally, I have been given a termination notice. I have one month time to clean up here. If ever I can be of service to you, please let me know." Wilson retorted, "Sorry to hear that news Jim. As you know, I am a fledgling attempting to spread my wings. If something develops I will let you know, but it is going to take some time."

Finishing the Mechanical Analytics contracts would provide some seed money for Wilson, but would also require a considerable amount of his time and effort. He could not let the MA effort disrupt preparation for his new company, Tribos Engineering. Thus, he would have to work extra hard to accomplish both goals of satisfying former customers and initiating the start of his company. One of the jobs to be completed was for NASA, and Wilson planned to visit Cleveland, where NASA Glenn was located, to discuss results of the project and determine if there might be additional contract opportunities. The trip would be supported by utilizing his own funds and would be independent of Mechanical Analytics.

That evening, Wilson discussed his plans with Maureen. She indicated "Wilson, I believe your plans are very good, but I think you should stretch your schedule. You are trying to do too much in a short period of time and you could end up sick. I think you should take it easy. I have confidence that you will get business and that we will be fine." Wilson digested her remarks and thought to himself that she was right and he would slow down somewhat. "I think you are right dear. I am trying to do too much all at once. I am going to set up a plan of attack that makes more sense and does not impose an impossible effort. Thanks for your critique, it was very helpful. Sometimes you need an outsider looking in to make things credible."

Wilson decided on spending a half day at Mechanical Analytics completing his projects and the remainder of the day (and part of the night) setting up and marketing his business. However, a 5 day work week was not contemplated.

Weekend work was required. The scheme appeared workable and could meet budgetary and time constraints.

Wilson's treks to Mechanical Analytics were distressing. The staff was in turmoil and was very upset with the bankruptcy. The group he was with was being sold to another organization, and for the time being they were to remain at their present quarters. The atmosphere was distracting and Wilson found it difficult to get his work done. He made sure his office door was closed so that he could isolate himself from the rest of the organization and concentrate on the task ahead. It was necessary to complete his reports at the facility because he had to refer to documents and drawings. He also had to coordinate with the Report Services group regarding report layout, proof reading, etc. As time elapsed he completed both reports that were sent on to sponsors. After he submitted his invoice to Mechanical Analytics, he was surprised to receive prompt payment. Subsequently he learned that the bankruptcy judge wanted all outstanding debits cleared up as quickly as possible and so his payment was made promptly. Wilson was not lacking in the marketing department as he worked diligently in the evening. He sent out over 100 marketing packets describing his capabilities and listing his prior projects and publications. He also mentioned his library of computer codes for doing analytical work.

Wilson learned that the group he worked with at Mechanical Analytics was being sold to a company called Investigative Research. They were a well-respected company and had been a worthy competitor to Mechanical Analytics on quite a few proposals. They did their best to solicit Wilson as an employee. That meant relocating down south and Wilson would have none of that. Maureen would definitely not approve. He was now committed to his own business at Tribos Engineering. The response to his marketing activity was quite good and he was able to obtain some small rotor dynamic contracts quickly. He made a trip to Cleveland to visit NASA Glenn to discuss his report on the buffer seal project and propose further work. The purpose of the buffer seal is to separate hydrogen and oxygen in a space engine. If allowed to communicate with each other, a severe explosion could occur. The work done at Mechanical Analytics considered a variety of seal concepts in a cursory manner. A preliminary selection was made that consisted of a seal that incorporated hydrostatic principles to levitate the seal so that it would not contact the rotating shaft and with helium exit paths to both the hydrogen and oxygen sides. Wilson presented a future course of action that included comprehensive analysis, design, manufacture and test. NASA was receptive and indicated that a task statement would be developed for a future

SBIR and Wilson was encouraged to respond. SBIR stands for Small Business Innovative Research and is a program designed for small businesses to present innovative ideas for solution to government research problems. Wilson left NASA encouraged, but he realized that he could not complete the seal program alone and he would need experimental facilities. Wilson could handle the analysis and design with Homer and Edgar's assistance, but manufacture and test could be a hang-up.

When Wilson returned home he decided to call the Sealall Company in Philadelphia. He had worked with Sealall before and they had the facilities to complete the missing pieces for the SBIR program. In particular, their manufacturing and testing equipment would be necessary ingredients. Wilson had to determine whether they would be willing to be a subcontractor to his fledging organization. The Sealall Company was owned by Paul Stanton and was not a public company. They had about 300 employees and as such was considered a small business by the government. Their size would be a plus for an SBIR contract. They produced many types of seals, but their main product was circumferential bearing compartment seals for jet engines and gas turbines. Sealall had excellent manufacturing and testing capability. Sealall mostly worked directly with engine manufacturers.

They were not well equipped to propose research directly with the government as required for an SBIR. Mr. Stanton was amenable to working with Wilson and Tribos Engineering, but it would depend upon the details as they surfaced. Wilson explained that there were two phases to an SBIR. Phase 1 is limited to around 100 thousand dollars and is thus restricted in scope. Wilson's tentative plan for Phase 1 would include analysis and design of the hydrostatic seal and a plan for Phase 2. Sealall's participation would be small in Phase 1. They would look over the manufacture requirements and approve the Phase 2 preliminary plan. The Phase 2 contract would be much larger than the Phase 1 and would entail manufacture and test. Sealall would have a major role if a Phase 2 contract was awarded. The funding for a Phase 2 would be in the $800,000 to $1,000,000 range. Paul Stanton was quite anxious to gain entrance to government research and indicated he looked forward to working with Wilson. Although Sealall would be a major sub-contractor, there were others that would have to be involved, at least for the Phase 2 effort. Namely a helium supply would be necessary for the testing phase. Contact would have to be made with a helium supplier and coordinated with Sealall since the helium tanks would be required to be installed at the Sealall facility. Wilson realized that a significant amount of effort would be required for proposal preparation, but he was anxious to proceed. He felt that he had good relations with NASA and he might be able to capitalize with a major R&D program and an SBIR award.

The next day Wilson met with Homer and they discussed design aspects of the hydrostatic seal and Wilson authorized Homer to start laying out the design. Wilson had a good idea of the general dimensions from the prior effort at Mechanical Analytics. Once a detailed layout was completed, Edgar would be contacted to complete the details and produce design drawings using his plotting facilities. Details however, would not be required for the forthcoming proposal, but would be implemented only after receipt of contract. For the proposal effort a layout of the design would suffice with explanation of its operation along with estimates of performance. If a Phase 1 contract was awarded, Wilson would complete computer studies that would detail performance.

THE ROTARY TABLE

Wilson received a call from Jason Terwilliger the CEO of Advanced Machine Tool (AMT) in Milwaukee, Wisconsin. "Mr. Shindler, I have read over your biography and capabilities, and I think that you might be able to help us on a project we intend to embark on. Could you possibly come to Milwaukee so that we could discuss the project? Of course your travel expenses will be compensated." Wilson replied "It sounds intriguing, and I will be happy to meet with you at your convenience".

Arrangements were made and Wilson found himself on the way to Milwaukee. At the office of AMT, he was cordially received by Mr. Terwilliger. After some small talk about family, and Wilson's plane ride etc., Mr. Terwilliger got down to business. "Mr. Shindler, I am intrigued by your background in gas bearings. As you probably know, our company has been building rotary tables for a long time. However, they have been of comparatively small size, 2 feet diameter being the largest. We use air bearings to avoid stick-slip problems and also to avoid the necessity for an external oil lubrication system. There are rotary table applications for much larger sizes, in the 6 to 7 foot diameter range. I am afraid that our conventional captured bearings would not work well for such large diameters. There would be difficulties in accepting thermal and centrifugal expansions for one thing and machining to very tight tolerances would be difficult. The requirements are not only for position accuracy, but also for high-speed operation. Do you think you might come up with a bearing system for such an application?" Wilson replied. "Let me have the parameter requirements of dimensions and operation and I can get back to you in two weeks' time with my assessment as to .probability and a potential configuration. I will need a purchase order for $10,000 plus expenses and I will get back to you in two weeks." Mr. Terwilliger replied, "Sounds good to me. I will arrange for the purchase order and have our chief engineer provide you with details. He will also take you to lunch. It was a pleasure meeting you and I look forward to what you come up with in two weeks."

Wilson had lunch with Charles Goodling, the chief engineer of the company. He was an amiable sort and the two got along rather well. During lunch, Wilson remarked, "I suppose Charles that you will be my liaison, if the project develops." Charles replied, "I am afraid not Wilson. Mr. Terwilliger runs a very tight ship. We are short of engineers and everyone, including me, is over loaded. My advice is to act as independently as possible, with a minimum of interaction, because everyone is so busy that there will be no one to really help you. I am going to provide you with some layout drawings, which should allow you to proceed to determine if there is a feasible solution. Then, in two weeks present your ideas to Mr. Terwilliger and he will decide whether you can move head long into the project. Before you leave today we will take a quick tour of the factory, so you get some idea of what we are all about. I would love to work with you on this project, but it is just not possible at this time."

Wilson was impressed with the factory tour and he noted that the engineering staff was indeed very busy. He left AMT with folded drawings that he fit into his briefcase and a purchase order for conceptual studies. He taxied to the airport and was soon on a plane back to New York. On the way home, Wilson wondered why Jason Terwilliger did not hire additional staff. He seemed to be placing unnecessary burdens on his existing staff, and Wilson thought that this would lead to inefficiencies in time.

Back home, Wilson contacted Homer and Edgar and set up a concept meeting to discuss the AMT problem. Wilson had some definite ideas on how to proceed. Gas bearings work at tight clearances, so that a captured design for a large table would not work. His concept consisted of a series of separate pads surrounding the circumference of the table. He chose the circumference of the table to install a radial bearing system rather than the drive shaft. The larger diameter would considerably increase stiffness and load capacity. Some pads would be fixed radially, and some would be free floating. The floating pads would be piston actuated with air pressure behind the pistons and in effect the floating pads would preload the fixed pads. The operating clearance would adjust automatically. The floating pad clearance would be a function of the pressure behind the pistons and the fixed pad clearances would be a function of the preload applied to them and the external load applied.

At 9 AM the next day, Wilson met with Homer and Edgar. He reviewed his trip to Milwaukee and his assignment regarding the large rotary table. They all studied the information provided by AMT, and then Wilson presented his solution sketches. For purposes of the two week feasibility study, Wilson wanted a few layouts to be completed. He considered 12 pads each of 30 degrees that would surround the circumference of the table. Wilson described that 6 of the 12 pads would be radially fixed and that 6 would be floating. He wanted sketches of the assembly and of the fixed and floating pad. He also wanted to show that the hydrostatic The advantages of the porous carbon are elimination of drilled orifices and their ability to accept high speed rubs. Schematic of the air pressure circuity for the entire table was also to be produced. For simplification purposes he wanted one air inlet to the entire table. In addition to radial containment by air bearings, Wilson suggested a more conventional air bearing in the axial or thrust direction. That bearing would consist of a donut shaped structure with a series of circumferential in let holes which would be fed through orifice restrictors. This bearing need only support the weight of the table structure. He instructed Homer to make some preliminary pencil sketches via his drafting board, which would be given to Edgar to make plotter produced more formal drawings. The plotted drawings were to contain Tribos Engineering labels to provide formality and ownership of the ideas presented. Both men understood their instructions and all would meet again in one week's time. Wilson, himself would make some preliminary computations by revising computer codes as necessary and producing approximate results.

Good progress was made in one weeks' time, and Wilson wanted all layouts completed by the following week. He stated that he would try to arrange a meeting with Mr. Terwilliger for the subsequent Monday, following completion of the layouts.

The meeting with Jason Terwilliger went very well. Mr. Terwilliger was impressed with the concept and he thought the ideas had addressed all the difficult problems that the application had surfaced. Jason then asked Wilson what was next on the agenda. Wilson replied "Next is to complete a comprehensive analysis and design drawings that would enable manufacture. I am not sure how far you want us to take this. Will ATM do the manufacture and test? How much should Tribos be involved after the design phase?" Terwilleger stated, "We are over loaded with work. I want Tribos to take this to the bitter end, where you will install a finished product on one of our large turntables". Wilson answered, "Then I would like to take this in stages. By the end of the week I could submit a quote and schedule for completing the design, and later on advise on manufacture and checkout." Terwilliger responded "That sounds good! We would like to move as soon as possible. Keep me advised of progress on a monthly basis. I don't need a formal report. An e-mail or telephone call will suffice. I think you are on the right track Wilson, and I am anxious to see how this all works out."

Wilson left ATM pleased with the results of the meeting, but somewhat concerned with the path ahead. Wilson thought, "If we have to do manufacture and test, then we will need a facility. Manufacture can be sub contracted, but Tribos would be required to do assembly and test. That means a facility plus additional labor. It also means immediate capital."

That evening he discussed the situation with Maureen. "When I left Mechanical Analytics, I thought I could be an independent consultant. My plan was to apply analysis and design, and I didn't think I would have to go beyond Homer and Edgar for outside assistance. Now the situation is mushrooming into hardware supply. It is a very big step, requiring additional staff, facilities and equipment. It is somewhat scary, but also challenging and interesting. Why can't I be the entrepreneur that builds a thriving organization? The rotary table project provides my entrance into building a big and profitable organization. Capital is the stumbling block." Maureen replied. "Wilson, the situation is exciting. You are being presented with a tremendous opportunity, and I have complete confidence in your ability to pull it off. We have been getting bank advertisements about Home Equity Loans, and that would be a good place to start."

The next day Wilson visited the TriCities bank where he and Maureen were customers for many years. They had both a checking and Money Market account and they also had paid off their home mortgage with the bank. Wilson talked to a manager and he applied for a $300,000 home equity loan which had an interest rate of 3.5%. Over a 10 year period, the monthly cost would be about $3000. This would be a good start. When he returned home, Wilson made a to-do list as follows:

- Propose design cost to ATM
- Look for a working facility
- Purchase office equipment for the facility
- Begin analysis of rotary table bearing system
- Begin design of rotary table bearing system
- Consider how to manufacture the rotary table bearing system.
- Be alert for NASA Request for Proposal.
- Consider hiring additional personnel for manufacture and test.
- Consider changing Tribos to a C corporation

When Wilson evaluated the list, it became apparent that he could not do all the tasks enumerated without help. He had Homer and Edgar in the fold, but he needed more, especially with non-technical tasks such as finding an adequate facility and obtaining office supplies and many other tasks. He looked in the phone book and obtained Jim Clairborne's, his old boss's telephone number. "Hello Jim, How is the job searching going?" Jim replied "Rather slowly. How about you Wilson?" "Things are moving rapidly for me, too rapidly. I could use some help and you came to mind. If you could come over to the house, I can explain the situation and how you might fit in. I can't offer anything permanent yet, but we could work on a contract basis and see what develops." Jim answered "I would love to work with you, Wilson and I can meet you at your convenience." A meeting date was established.

Wilson then sent an e-mail off to Jason Terwilliger stating that the design of the air bearing system could be completed in 3 month's at an estimated cost of $100,000. Wilson expected to receive a purchase order shortly. He then called Homer and told him that he wanted to start on the design the following day and to meet with him tomorrow.

The meeting with Jim Clairborne went quite well. They agreed upon a contract price structure, and Jim was to submit invoices on a bi-weekly basis. Wilson explained that for much of the work to be done, there was no one to delegate to. He felt that he was the only one who could accomplish certain tasks, such as the computer analysis. Therefore, he needed someone else to accomplish the many administrative tasks. Jim commented "I really think that I could be of assistance and I look forward to the challenge." Wilson replied "Good! The first task is to find a facility so that we could get everyone in one place. We will also need furniture, office supplies, and some equipment such as a drafting plotter. Perhaps we could purchase Edgar's plotter if it fits our needs and he is willing to sell. We will also have to establish a salary and benefit schedule. I also anticipate hiring additional personnel for manufacture and test. Jim, there is lots of work to be done and if we do it right I have confidence we will be successful. Please keep in contact with me as considered necessary. I expect a loan approval from the bank shortly that should maintain us for a while. Once we get into manufacture we will probably need to increase the loan." Jim replied, "OK Wilson, I am anxious to begin." Wilson felt that Jim had a good command of the situation and that he could trust his judgment.

The next day Wilson met with Homer to discuss the design. "I am thinking about 12 thirty degree pads surrounding the circumference of the table. Six pads would be fixed and six pads would be floating. All the pads would be made of porous carbon contained by a steel retainer. The porous media should be about an inch and a half thick. The air should be supplied through one connection. The original preliminary sketches should be a good place to start. Let's get a more detailed layout going and have Edgar draw up the details. In the meantime I will initiate computer analysis to determine performance characteristics. Incidentally, Jim Clairborne is helping us and looking for a facility where we can assemble a system and do checkout tests. Once that happens we can all work in one place and be employees of Tribos Engineering." Homer responded, "Sounds good to me." Wilson was hoping that Edgar felt the same way.

Wilson began his analysis of the air bearing system. His plan was to analyze a single pad over a range of clearances. For each clearance he would characterize performance parameters, such as flow, load capacity, stiffness, damping and friction. Then he would write an assembly code using the pre-calculated performance characteristics of each pad as a function of its clearance. Complete performance would be generated either as a function of table displacement or as a function of the machining load applied to the table. Wilson found the project fascinating and was quite anxious to proceed. However, it did occur to Wilson that the time frame would not allow a linear sequence of analysis, design, manufacture and test as a research project might dictate. The analysis alone would easily consume the three month time frame allotted for the completion of a design and that would require Wilson's full time that he could not possibly devote to just the analytical phase.. He had to be involved in the design process as well as originating a facility and obtaining manufacturing sub- contractors. . Wilson decided to trust his judgment concerning the final configuration and proceed with the design as given to Homer and let the analysis follow at a later date. He would use empirical methods as much as possible.

The following day Wilson heard from Jim Clairborne. "Wilson, I found an interesting possibility that we should check out in more detail. The company presently occupying the space is moving south to join with their headquarters and they have been renting here. It is very nice with offices up front and a large garage area in the back. They are also amenable to selling their office equipment." The possibility excited Wilson and he replied, "I will meet you tomorrow to have a look."

The next day, Wilson met Jim at the proposed site. Wilson was very impressed. He inquired, "Do you know what the landlord wants for rent?" Jim responded, "He wants $5000 per month, but he is willing to defer payment for 6 months so that we have a chance to begin making money by shipping product." "That is great Jim, let us close the deal as far as the facility is concerned. What about the office supplies?" Jim replied, "They want $6000 for everything. I think it is a good deal. Replacement costs would probably be closer to double that amount." Wilson looked around and inspected the furniture and file cabinets as best he could. His inspection was restricted because the equipment was still in use. However, things looked pretty good and Wilson agreed to the sale. Jim commented, "We can move in in three weeks. The present residents are in the process of gathering belongings and will be moving out in two weeks. The landlord said he would need a week to clean up and then we could move in." Wilson retorted, "Everything sounds great to me. Good job Jim. Pretty soon Tribos Engineering will have a place of their own. Please take care of all the details. Incidentally, we had better set up a pay structure so that we all can get paid.'" Jim replied, "For the time being, since we don't have an accounting group, we can outsource to a payroll outfit that will take care of everything."

Things were moving along smoothly. Jim attended to the administrative tasks and Wilson concentrated on the design process and the analytical computer code. The move to the new building would interrupt things, but only for a few days. The design was proceeding well and it was time to start thinking about manufacture. Once again, Jim came to the rescue. Mechanical Analytics outsourced most of their manufacture and Jim was familiar with the shops that MA used. He contacted several shops, but needed to wait for the completion of the design to obtain quotations. After several weeks, the design was completed to Wilson's satisfaction. He sent the drawings on to ATM with an invoice for the design phase. He mentioned to ATM, that he was working on a quotation for manufacture, which he would send in the next several weeks. There was one area of manufacture that needed special attention. The porosity of the graphite will probably not be uniform throughout the porous pad structure. To compensate for differences in porosity, the surface can be impregnated with a resin. Different amounts of resin are used over the surface to provide a uniform resistance to flow. A special flow device is necessary to measure the flow for a given supply pressure over different portions of the surface. Impregnation fluid is added at the measured location until the flow reaches the required value. Homer was working on the design of the flow device. Wilson discussed this manufacturing procedure with Jim and he commented, "We are going to need at least three technicians for manufacture and checkout. Perhaps we can hire some that may have been laid off by Mechanical Analytics. Please look into it Jim. Frank Klamberg was especially adapt at the impregnation procedure to graphite. Let's see if we can hire him. Also, we will need someone to monitor our manufacturing subcontractors."

As time progressed, things were falling into place. Manufacturing subcontractors were selected and a quotation was forwarded to AMT. The cost not only included the cost to produce the components, but also the cost for in house checkout and assembly and test at the ATM facility. The total cost was near one million dollars and Wilson required an advance of one half. Jason Terwilliger paid without a whimper; he was very anxious to get the gas bearing supported large rotary table. He knew there was big business out there and he provided Wilson with a large nest egg for his fledgling company. Wilson found the enterprise very exciting.

Jim Clairborne had hired Gerry Albertelli to monitor subcontracting manufacture. Since Tribos did not yet have inspection equipment, Gerry was responsible for inspections at the manufacturer's facility to ensure parts were within drawing specifications. Frank Klamberg was also hired and his major responsibility was to impregnate the carbon elements to provide a uniform and specified resistance to flow.

Soon parts began to flow into the plant and procedures were established for in house assembly and preliminary testing. Compressed air bottles were ordered to supply pressurized air to the impregnation rig and for checking out each graphite pad. An impregnation resin was chosen and a barrel was supplied to the plant. The resin was labeled C-5 and contained all the desired characteristics of penetration, high temperature capability, quick setting and low wear to rubbing. Procedures were established for each manufacturing and assembly process and the work was proceeding in an organized manner. Wilson was proud of the staff, not only for their work ethic, but also for their ingenuity and thoughtful application. Tribos had a staff of 10 persons and each was dedicated to the success of the mission. After impregnation, each pad was assembled in a checkout rig that applied a load to a pressurized pad. The pad clearance and flow was measured and recorded. There was remarkable consistency between all 12 pads mainly because of the impregnation job accomplished by Frank.

During evening hours, Wilson worked on his assembly computer program at home and knowing the results of the single pad tests he could now predict the performance of the assembly. He was able to ball park the clearance of each pad, the stiffness of the assembly and the total flow requirements. Wilson believed the performance parameters were good and he was anxious to run performance tests of the complete bearing system at AMT to verify his predictions.

Soon all parts were delivered and assembly checkout at the Tribos facility completed. It was time to pack up and deliver the bearing installation to AMT. The plan was to rent a truck and drive to Milwaukee. Wilson, Frank and Robert Carpone were to go. Robert was a recent addition to the Technician Staff. He provided brute strength to the trio, which they might need in Milwaukee. With three drivers, The AMT plant in Milwaukee could be reached in three days.

The truck left Tribos from New York about noon time and was headed for Wisconsin with all the bearing components aboard. The trek to AMT was long and arduous, but uneventful, which was considered good. The driving was split three ways and was done continuously for 12 hour shifts. Stops were made for eating and sleeping at motels. Arrival at AMT was made about noon time on the third day. The afternoon was spent unloading the system components. Then Wilson, Frank and Robert went out for dinner and retired to their motel for the evening. The next day, after an early breakfast, they motored to the plant and began the process of unpacking the system components and installing them on the test rotary table that was made available. AMT personnel assisted in the assembly process and by the end of working hours the assembly was complete. Energizing and preliminary testing was to begin the following day.

The next day the air pressure hookup was completed early that morning. The system was designed for 100 pounds per square inch (psi) supply pressure. The inlet control valve was opened and the pressure set at 100 psi. Then the rotary table came to life. All porous pad were energized and the table was supported by a bed of very stiff air. Wilson gasped at the sight and took great pleasure in witnessing what was before him. A great deal of Tribos effort went into the bearing system and to see it energized and supporting the table as designed was very gratifying. Tribos had established a test plan during the design process and it was now time to implement the plan. Feeler gages were used on several pads to determine the clearance under operating conditions. Both the floating and fixed pad clearances were as designed. The first operational test was to establish position accuracy. Positions were determined by AMT controllers on the rotary table. The position accuracy was flawless without any stick slip which was characteristic of other bearing systems. The position tests were applied and monitored by AMT personnel and they were impressed with the accuracy of the air bearing supported table. The position tests lasted most of the afternoon with rotations in both directions from less than one degree to three hundred degrees. High speed tests were slated for the following day.

The next morning, the table was rotated at various speeds. The speed increment was 100 revolutions per minute and each speed was held for 10 minutes. The maximum operating speed was 3600 revolutions per minute, .which was held for two hours, and the elapsed time consumed the working day. Rotations applied both centrifugal and thermal growth to the table, which was easily accommodated by the floating piston system. The bearing system worked perfectly without any signs of distress. Tomorrow a dummy work piece would be secured to the table and simulated machining loads would be applied. The loads would consist of simulated turning and milling operations.

The next morning, load test were conducted and there was hardly any noticeable movement of the table, because of the high stiffness of the system. In the afternoon several pads were disassembled for inspection and they showed no signs of distress or dimensional change. Jason Terwilliger then appeared and congratulated Wilson on the success of the acceptance testing. "Wilson, I congratulate you on the trouble free system that you supplied. Our plans include the sale of many tables and I want you to continue to supply us. There is plenty of business for both of us." Wilson replied "Thank you Jason. I am very gratified that the testing went on without a hitch, and we look forward to supplying many more bearing systems. I realize they may not be all the same size, but we are prepared to accommodate what you specify. We will also provide a Tribos representative at this plant for liaison and instructional purposes." Jason retorted, "That sounds great Wilson. We look forward to a long and profitable relationship."

On the drive home Wilson asked Robert Carpone if he would be the Tribos representative in Milwaukee. He would receive salary plus expenses and every two weeks he would be allowed flight pay to travel home for the weekend. Robert who was single without serious relationships in New York agreed whole heartily and looked forward to the adventure.

The ensuing days were busy with production. Wilson added three more technicians and a computer designer to the staff. Also, some machine tool equipment, namely lathes and milling machines were purchased on the used equipment market, so that a model shop was being formulated. The one big problem with the Tribos organization was that they had only one big customer. It was important that the organization spread out to other companies. Wilson had discussions with Jim Clairborne about seeking out other opportunities utilizing the technology developed under the Rotary Table concepts. However, before a marketing effort could materialize, Tribos received the Request for Proposal (RFP} for a Helium Purge Seal from NASA. Originally, Wilson planned to work with the Sealall Company on the purge seal because, at that time, he was an independent consultant and he needed facilities for manufacture and test. However, now that he had an organization, Wilson felt that he could handle the project without a major subcontractor. He gave a call to Paul Stanton at Sealall, "Paul, we have received the RFP from NASA on the purge seal, but conditions have changed since we last spoke. I am no longer an independent consultant, but business conditions have enabled me to build a fledging organization and I believe that we can handle the project on our own. In order to expand our company we must be able to handle these kinds of projects on our own without a major subcontractor." Paul replied, "Wilson, I am somewhat disappointed, but I can understand your position. I am going to have our people look at the RFP to see if there is any interest. We are so busy now that I doubt we will have the personnel to bid, but I wish you the best of luck".

BETWEEN THE EYES

In Wilson's office he and Homer were brainstorming ideas for the NASA proposal. They were considering a hydrostatic seal with an inverted T crossection. A circumferential row of orifices located in the midplane would feed the clearance space between the seal and the shaft. The helium would flow in both directions toward the hydrogen and oxygen sides. Tapered land secondary seals would seal the vertical sides of the inverted T. When pressurized the tapered land secondary seals would form a clearance between the tapered land and inverted T. In addition to seal design, the plan was to design a test rig for Phase 2 testing. Wilson and Homer were about to consider the rig design when they were alerted to a knock at the office door. Jim Clairborne entered with a stapled set of papers in his hand. He laid the paper in front of Wilson's desk and related "Thought you might be interested in this." Wilson looked at the papers in front of him and he could hardly believe what he saw. It was a patent for the rotary table gas bearing system with the author being Charles Goodling, the chief engineer of AMT, and of course the patent was assigned to AMT. There was no question that the wrongful patent was the work of Jason Terwilliger. Charles Goodling was not involved with the project at all, yet Terwilliger chose to name him the inventor. Wilson felt the blood rush to his head and his face turned a deep red. He turned to Jim, and said "We cannot let this illegitimate patent stand. It gives AMT ownership of our bearing system including all of the additional applications that might ensue. We have to challenge the patent. Homer will you continue to consider concepts for the seal proposal, and please excuse me while I make a phone call." Homer understood and retired to his office. Wilson asked Jim to stick around as he dialed Jason Terwilliger's number. "Hello, Jason, this is Wilson Shindler from Tribos Engineering." Terwilliger responded, "Hello Wilson, what can I do for you." Wilson then related, "I have before me a patent disclosure concerning the large rotary table bearing system, authored by Charles Goodling and assigned to AMT." Jason retorted, "Oh yes. We decided to file for patent under AMT authorship as it makes us look good to the board of directors, and it provides us protection against possible competition." Wilson had difficulty containing himself as he replied, "Jason you know as well as I that the patent is illegitimate because it has the wrong inventor. I am the creator of the bearing system, and Charles Goodling had nothing to do with it." Jason retorted, "That might be true Wilson but I wanted the idea to be created by an AMT employee, as I said that helps our appearance before the board. After all, we are providing considerable business for Tribos

Engineering." Wilson replied, "If you had discussed a patent application with me, mutually agreeable arrangements could have been made to protect the system for rotary tables, and proper authorship could have been included. As things stand now, I have no recourse but to challenge the patent." Jason chuckled, and replied, "Wilson, it costs a lot of money to challenge a patent. Why don't you keep supplying us the system like a good fellow and leave the patent alone?" At this point, Wilson slammed the receiver down and did his best to settle his mind. He then turned to Jim, "I am going to do whatever I can to challenge that patent." Jim replied, "I know how you feel Wilson, but remember AMT is our best customer." Then Wilson retorted, "AMT would not go anywhere else. We will be in the unenviable position of suing our best customer, but it must be done. You must know some patent attorneys from your experience with Mechanical Analytics. Please provide me with names, phone numbers, etc. so that I could arrange a meeting." Then Jim offered, "Jeremy Patterson is an excellent patent attorney and a nice guy. I'll dig out his number from my contact file."

Arrangements were made for Wilson to meet with Jeremy Patterson in two weeks' time. In the interim, Wilson worked diligently on the NASA seal proposal. The proposal was for a phase 1 Small Business Innovative Research Program (SBIR), which was limited to a contract value of about 100 thousand dollars. The Phase 1 plan was to complete the design and analysis of the seal and to configure a test rig. Complete design of the rig would be accomplished in Phase 2. Manufacture and test would also be conducted in a Phase 2 program, which had a much higher dollar limit, close to a million dollars. Wilson was considering another twist in the hydrostatic seal design. A porous carbon cylindrical ring could be fixed to the interior of the inverted T section and supplied at portions of its exterior with the pressure to be sealed. The modulus of elasticity of carbon is considerably less than steel and hydrostatic pressure would deflect the carbon away from the shaft. The net result would be smaller clearances and less flow. Also, the carbon would be more tolerant of high speed rubs if they occurred. The proposal would discuss the carbon feature and propose analysis and design along with a standard hydrostatic design. Wilson felt that the addition of an innovative concept that the graphite carbon provided would be welcome by the NASA reviewers. The proposal formulation was in good order and Wilson set out to complete the write up with the help of Jim Clairborne. Wilson's main thrust, however, was the illegitimate patent from AMT and he was anxious to determine what he could do to attack that problem.

<u>RECOURSE</u>

In two weeks' time, Wilson met with Jeremy Patterson, the patent lawyer recommended by Jim. Wilson brought along all his notes, sketches, etc. He explained to Mr. Patterson, "I was called in by Jason Terwilliger to consider a solution for a gas bearing support system for a large rotary table. The captured arrangement used on smaller tables would not work because excessive clearance would be necessary to accommodate centrifugal and thermal expansion. Gas bearings require low clearance to produce good load capacity and stiffness. I came up with the idea of a series of fixed and floating pads as indicated in my hand written sketches. Mr. Terwilliger gave me the OK to proceed with development. I also decided to utilize porous carbon pads as they provide their own hydrostatic restrictor and are more forgiving of high speed rubs." Mr. Patterson inquired "Is there anything that Mr. Terwilliger does not know about that is exclusive to your invention?" Wilson replied "Yes there is. The porosity of most carbons are not uniform and can vary significantly across the pad surface. We have developed an exclusive impregnation process with C-5 resin, and the method to apply it, to obtain a uniform and desired restriction to flow over the surface of the pad. Mr. Terwilliger was never interested in how we made the pads. He just cared about delivery of workable systems. Impregnation is essential to proper working order of a pad." At the end of the description, Mr. Patterson remarked "You may have a chance to contest the patent. It is usually a difficult enterprise. I am sure Mr. Terwilliger will have ammunition to defend his position. Are you willing to spend $50,000 to $100,000 to invalidate the patent when I estimate the odds for winning to be 50%?" Wilson gasped at the amount of money involved. He replied, "I need to give that decision more thought and I will get back to you in several days. Thank you for your attention."

Back at the plant, Wilson conferred with Jim Clairborne. "There must be a way to contest the patent without digging into our coffers. It is very important to invalidate the AMT patent since it could seriously impair our ability to promote other applications of porous hydrostatic bearings. I know that you have been considering a multitude of applications where our concept can be applied." Jim considered Wilson's comment and replied, "Have you thought about going to an AMT competitor, who would be happy to see the patent overturned." Wilson thought for a moment and retorted, "Jim that is a brilliant idea. There must be companies who would love to see the AMT patent thrown out, so that they could get into the ball game. One of their close competitors is Rotating Table Machines (RTM), I will give them a call."

The call went through to RTM and as expected, Wilson first talked to a receptionist. "Hello, my name is Wilson Shindler. I am the president of Tribos Engineering, and we supply the bearing systems for large rotary tables to Advanced Manufacturing Technology (AMT). I would like to speak to your CEO, Mr. Josh Worthington about a very important matter." The receptionist told Wilson, "Please hold Mr. Shindler. I will check to see if Mr. Worthington is available." After a considerable amount of time and background noise Wilson was finally put in contact with Mr. Worthington. "Hello Mr. Shindler. We here at RTM have heard a lot about you." Wilson liked those words as he felt that he wasn't communicating cold turkey. "Well I am glad you know of me Mr. Worthington. I am calling about Patent No 20141234 assigned to Advanced Manufacturing Technology." Worthington replied, "Yes, we are familiar with that patent, and it is very disappointing to us that AMT will have exclusive rights to that technology for large rotary tables." Wilson retorted, "Mr. Worthington, that patent is invalid. I am the inventor of the bearing system not an AMT employee, Charles Goodling, as the patent specifies. I could use the help of RTM to fight the patent." Worthington retorted, "We had nothing to do with the bearing technology, so how can we be involved?" Wilson continued, "I understand that, but my company is a fledging organization and we do not have the resources to fight the patent. We are requesting that RTM, bankroll the legal fees involved. If the patent is made invalid then RTM can avail themselves of the technology and in any event destroy AMT's exclusivity claims." It took some time before Mr. Worthington replied, "Mr. Shindler, I understand the situation, but before we can get involved we would like more proof of your claims. I suggest we have a meeting here so that you could explain your claims." Wilson answered, "That would be fine with me. I can bring all documentation concerning the bearing system."

Three days later Wilson was on a plane headed for Portland, Oregon where RTM was headquartered. He arrived at the plant around 4:00 PM and was immediately escorted to a meeting room where three RTM representatives were waiting. Josh Worthington, the CEO, Bob Allen, Chief Engineer and Bryce Morgan their patent attorney. Wilson was asked about his trip and he accepted a cup of coffee. The initiative for the meeting was Wilson's claim of patent infringement, so the floor was his. Wilson began his presentation, 'First, I would like to advise you gentlemen of my background so I brought along biographical information and a list of my publications. For the past ten years, I have been working with gas bearings and I am considered an expert in the field by my peers. About one year ago, the company I worked for. Mechanical Analytics declared bankruptcy. The declaration was due to mismanagement at the top. The engineering staff was very viable with research projects from government and industry. Most of the engineering staff was to be sold to another company but I opted out and decided to go into my own consulting business. As part of a marketing effort, I sent the information that I just gave you to many industrial organizations. One of the responses I received was from Jason Terwilliger of Advanced Manufacturing Technology (AMT). He suggested that we meet to discuss an application he had in mind. When we met his interest was in the development of a gas bearing system for a large table. AMT had tried a captured bearing arrangement, but the clearance required to accept centrifugal and thermal distortions was too large and the large clearance diminished load capacity and required excessive flow. I went home and produced my first sketch of the floating pad concept. Here are copies of the initial sketch with a date clearly stamped on it with my signature. The concept uses a series of floating and fixed pads that are individually fed with air. The idea allows small clearance operation and ability to accept thermal and centrifugal growth and still maintain the small clearances required for good air bearing operation. I also decided to use porous carbon pads that eliminates the use of drilled orifices and can accommodate high speed rubs if they occur. The concept was approved by Mr. Terwilliger and he gave the go ahead for my company, Tribos Engineering to develop the concept. We had great success and we now are supplying bearing systems to AMT on a continuous and exclusive basis." The meeting continued for some time with the RTM personnel asking technical questions, which were readily answered. Some detailed technical data was withheld by Wilson for proprietary reasons. Bryce Morgan, the patent attorney commented, "It seems, Mr. Shindler that the only piece of evidence that indicates you as the inventor is the preliminary sketch that you have showed us. That may be easily overcome by Mr. Terwilliger." Wilson replied "That may be true Mr. Morgan, but there is much more to it than that. I have intimate knowledge of every detail of the design that AMT does not and I believe that AMT can be tripped up when specific questions are asked. Mr. Terwilliger was not much interested in details. He just wanted me to provide a workable bearing system. Their Chief Engineer, Mr. Charles Goodling is the designated inventor on the patent, and he did not have anything to do with the project. He was busy engineering the small table systems. The patent itself is full of incorrect descriptions and claims that can be contested in court." Discussions continued for a while and finally Mr. Worthington interjected, "Wilson, we appreciate your visit. We should have a decision for you in a few days. Bob Allen will take you to dinner and your hotel." The meeting ended

The following day, Wilson returned to New York, not knowing whether RTM would agree to proceed, but he felt that the effort was worth the chance. On the plane ride back, Wilson studied the patent carefully and in his mind conjured up questions that could possibly trip up AMT personnel who were ignorant of many of the design aspects of the bearing system.

The day after returning, Mr. Worthington phoned Wilson. "Wilson, we were quite impressed with your presentation the other day and we believe that you are the true inventor. It would greatly benefit us if the patent was ruled invalid since that would enable us to get into the large rotary table business. We are willing to take the chance that you could win in court. Bryce Morgan feels that you should use a patent attorney that is in close proximity as intimate contact would probably be necessary. You can send his bills to my attention and we will see that you are compensated." Wilson replied, "That sounds great Josh. My patent attorney is Jeremy Patterson, who is well reputed and I have confidence he will do an excellent job." Worthington retorted, "Best of luck Wilson."

Wilson immediately called Jeremy Patterson, "Jeremy, I have made arrangements for financing the challenge and I would like to get started immediately." Patterson retorted, "All right Wilson, but before we get started you will have to sign some paper work, mainly a contract between us." Wilson replied, "I will be right over Jeremy, and I can brief you on my funding backup."

Wilson hurried over to Jeremy Patterson's office, signed the necessary paper work and briefed Jeremy on his trip to RTM. Now, the challenge was on. During the ensuing days, Jeremy Patterson filed the necessary briefs with the appropriate courts and began preparing for a court encounter with AMT. He had numerous communications with Wilson and he felt that between him and Wilson, they were as prepared as possible for the confrontation to come. Some two months had passed since the challenge began when Jeremy Patterson received a call from AMT's patent attorney, John Oliver. "Hello Jeremy. John Oliver here. I am representing AMT in your patent challenge. We would like to discuss a settlement rather than go to court. Would you client agree?" Patterson answered, "The only settlement my client would agree to is that the patent become invalid. He is absolutely convinced that he is the inventor and he is willing to take his challenge to court. "Oliver replied, "Well keep the offer on tap in case your client might change his mind. It might be worth a lot of money to him." Patterson retorted, "I'll let him know, but I believe you are wasting your time." As Patterson predicted, Wilson would have nothing to do with a settlement. His only interest now was to wait for the court proceedings where he could confront the AMT representatives. Jeremy Patterson estimated a two month time frame before the case was put on the docket and a subsequent two to three week period before the case would get to court. In the interim period, Wilson learned that his company, Tribos Engineering had won the first phase, of the helium buffer seal SBIR contract. This program would keep Wilson busy as he and Homer would come up with seal designs and a test rig design, which would hopefully be constructed during a Phase 2 contract. Two versions of the inverted T seal design were to be considered. The first used high density carbon with drilled orifices. The second used a metal backing with a porous carbon insert. Wilson busied himself with computer predictions of performance for both configurations, while Homer concentrated on the design. In the back of Wilson's mind was the Phase 2 Program as it would determine proof of concept through rigorous testing. The phase 1 program was to be completed in 6 months so a concentrated effort was necessary. After two months into the seal program, Wilson received a call from Jeremy Patterson. "We are on the court docket, and for some reason, they are in a hurry to clear it. Our court appointment is two weeks from tomorrow". This news was startling to Wilson as he had to juggle the patent challenge with all his other work including the seal contract and porous bearing production. His principal priority was the patent challenge, which would take him out of town for at least a week. Wilson hoped he could work at night, with his laptop computer, on the seal program wherever he might happen to be. Arrangements could be made for computer communication with Homer.

The next day Wilson met with Jeremy Patterson the patent attorney to plot strategy. It would be up to them to prove that Charles Goodling was not the inventor of the bearing system. After many hours of deliberating, a strategy was developed and it depended on calling two witnesses, Jason Terwilliger and Charles Goodling.

Since the case involved two states, New York and Wisconsin, the trial was to be held in a federal court in the Southern District of New York. Wilson and Jeremy Patterson traveled to the city and quartered in a hotel near the court house. The trial began at 10AM the next morning. The trial was not before a jury but was presided over by a judge who had the power to make guilty or not decisions. The presiding judge was Jerimiah Huston a tall strapping man whose height was 6 feet 5 inches and he weighed 250 pounds. He was a basketball star at Duke University and a brilliant scholar as well. Mechanical Engineering was his under graduate degree and he graduated near the top of his class. After graduation, he reversed course and decided to go into law. The combination of engineering and law made him ideally suited to preside over patent cases. He completed his law degree at Duke Law School and graduated Cum Laude. After graduation he returned to his native New York and passed, with honors, the bar exam there. He practiced patent law for ten years and five years ago was appointed as a federal judge.

The bailiff introduced the judge to a standing assembly. The judge sat down behind his bench followed by the trial participants and the spectators. The trial was on! The judge asked Jeremy Patterson, "Do you have some opening remarks?" Patterson replied "Yes your honor. We will prove that the patent in question is invalid, and that the true inventor is Mr. Wilson Shindler who sits at my side and not Mr. Charles Goodling who is named on the patent. Advance Manufacturing Technology (AMT) recognized the business potential of a large rotary table supported on air bearings. The air bearings would permit excellent position accuracy, because they avoided stick slip problems with other bearing systems. The bearing system would also allow high speed machining operation a definite advantage particularly to the aerospace industry. AMT tried to utilize the bearing systems used on their smaller rotary tables, which consisted of a captured hydrostatic system. However, when applied to large rotary tables the system failed. To accommodate centrifugal and thermal expansions of the table, necessary clearances were too high for air bearing support. Mr. Jason Terwilliger, CEO of AMT, then called on the services of Wilson Shindler, a gas bearing expert, to provide a workable air bearing support system for large rotary tables. Mr. Shindler than conceived the floating piston arrangement that has enjoyed tremendous success for the application. There is no doubt that Mr. Shindler is the true inventor of the floating piston, porous bearing system and we will prove that at this trial." The defense lawyer, Mr. William Buttons also opened and remarked. "Advanced Manufacturing Technology, AMT, knew the potential for an air bearing large rotary table, and invented the idea of the floating piston concept that has enjoyed tremendous success. They hired Tribos Engineering and in particular, Mr. Wilson Shindler to implement the concepts of AMT. Therefore, the charges against the validity of the patent is in itself invalid." Judge Huston then asked Mr. Patterson to call his first witness. Mr. Patterson called Jason Terwilliger to the stand. Mr. Terwilliger took the oath to tell the truth and nothing but the truth and sat down in the witness box. Patterson proceeded.

"Mr. Terwilliger, please state your name and affiliation." Terwilliger responded, "My name is Jason Terwilliger and I am the CEO of Advanced Manufacturing Technology."

Patterson: "What is your connection to the floating piston patent?"

Terwilliger: "We had great interest in a large rotary table supported on air bearings. We tried using our conventional captured system, but the necessary clearance to accommodate centrifugal and thermal expansion was too high resulting in excessive flow and poor stiffness. I met with the engineering staff and tasked them to come up with a solution and they produced the floating piston arrangement presently being used."

Patterson: "How did Wilson Shindler fit into the picture?"

Terwilliger: "Mr. Shindler, who was starting his own company, sent me information on his background and capabilities. He is considered a gas bearing expert and I asked him to produce the floating piston system as our staff was 100% occupied with other projects."

Patterson: "Did you provide Mr. Shindler with the necessary documentation to produce the air bearing system?"

Terwilliger: "No, we provided the table interface, but everything else was done on a verbal basis."

Patterson: "Isn't it true Mr. Terwilliger that you called Mr. Shindler, because you did not have a solution to the large table problem and you requested him to provide a solution? Remember Mr. Terwilliger you are under oath and Perjury is a serious offense."

Terwilliger: "No, we presented to Wilson, the floating piston concept, verbally."

Patterson: "Mr. Terwilliger, I am going to show you some sketches prepared by Mr. Shindler that clearly describe the floating piston system. There is a series of five sketches. Please note Mr. Shindler's signature and the date on each sketch. Judge I would like to introduce these sketches into evidence. Mr. Terwilliger, does AMT have any documentation concerning the floating piston system that predates these sketches?"

Terwilliger: "No we do not. Everything we had was done on a verbal basis."

Patterson: "Who verbalized with Mr. Shindler?"

Terwilliger: "It was Charles Goodling the inventor of the system."

Patterson: "No more questions, your honor."

Judge Huston interjected, "It is quite unusual, Mr. Terwilliger to not have any documentation describing the system that your patent considers." There was no response from Mr. Terwilliger.

The attorneys for AMT declined to question Terwilliger further as they felt that he could do more damage than good. Then, Jeremy Patterson called Charles Goodling to the stand. Your honor we request that Mr. Wilson Shindler be permitted to interrogate Mr. Goodling as he is directly challenging Mr. Goodling's patent." The judge agreed as long as the questioning was conducted properly.

Charles Goodling did not look like a confident witness. He was obviously very nervous about having to testify. When he took his oath he mumbled his "I do".

Shindler: "Hello Charles, it is nice to see you again. Charles what is the no load pad clearance when the system is energized?"

Goodling: "The general rule of thumb is 1 mil per radius. So for a 6 foot table the radius is 36 inches and the clearance would be 0.036 inches."

Shindler: "Charles, please look at this load capacity data taken during testing at Tribos Engineering. At a clearance of 0.036 inches and a supply pressure of 100 psig the load capacity for all practical purposes is zero. The system could not operate at that clearance. Judge I would like to offer in as evidence this load capacity test data." The judge agreed and the data was accepted into the trial documents. "Is it not true true Charles, that the floating piston concept allows the pads to operate at an optimum clearance of about 0.002 inches?"

Goodling: "I guess so."

Shindler: "Isn't it also true that the floating piston concept allows accommodation of centrifugal and thermal expansion even though the pads operate at a small clearance?"

Goodling: "If you say so."

Shindler: "Charles, what is your experience with porous carbon bearing pads?"

Goodling: "Most of the air bearings I deal with use steel pads. I really have no experience with porous carbon pads."

Shindler: "How come they were identified in your patent?"

Goodling: "Mr. Terwilliger told me to include them."

Shindler: "What are the advantages of using hydrostatic porous carbon pads?"

Goodling: "I do not believe they have any advantages over steel pads."

Shindler: "Isn't it true that the porous medium provides its own restrictor so that drilling orifices is not necessary,

Also, isn't it true that the porous carbon can withstand high speed rubs better than steel pads?"

Goodling: "If you say so."

By this time Judge Huston was getting very fidgety, about Goodling's lack of knowledge and his somewhat blasé attitude toward the questions addressed to him. Meanwhile Wilson Shindler considered that the time was ripe to impose the clincher.

Shindler: "Mr. Goodling, what is the purpose of the C-5 resin that is impregnated into the surface of the pads?"

Goodling: "I do not k now what you are talking about. I have never heard of C-5 resin."

Shindler; "Isn't it true Mr. Goodling that the porosity of the pads are inconsistent and in order to provide the desired downstream pressure a resin is impregnated at the surface, in calibrated amounts, to provide the design pressure drop through the pads? Your honor, I would like to introduce the impregnation procedure as an exhibit to the record."

Goodling: "I am not familiar with the C-5 resin or the impregnation process."

By this time Judge Huston was exasperated. He interjected, "Mr. Goodling, you do not seem to know very much about your own invention." Goodling responded, "Judge, the floating piston system is not my invention. I had very little to do with the entire project and I do not know very much about the system. I did not want my name on the patent, but Mr. Terwilliger insisted."

When Judge Huston heard those words, he slammed his gavel down on the bench and declared. "This case is over. The patent is invalid by virtue of erroneous inventor. Furthermore, the AMT Company forfeits all rights to exclusivity of the floating piston gas bearing system."

When Wilson heard the decision, he was ecstatic. He and Jeremy Patterson congratulated each other and Wilson quipped, "Jeremy, we better get started on a patent application, for the floating piston system, only this time with the true inventor, mainly me." Patterson was very agreeable and answered, "Wonderful idea. We will get started immediately." On the way out of the courtroom, Wilson and Patterson encountered Charles Goodling. Wilson shook his hand and said, "Charles, it took a lot of courage for you to do what you did today. If you are punished for your honesty, there will always be a job waiting for you at Tribos." Goodling replied, "I wasn't about to commit perjury for Jason Terwilliger. I believe Mr. Terwilliger will be in more trouble than me. The board of directors is losing patience with him. The staff have been complaining that Terwilliger does not hire and he is driving everyone too hard. In any event, I learned a lot about your system today and it is extremely interesting and innovative. I am hoping we get a chance to work together in the future."

When Wilson returned home he called Josh Worthington of Rotating Table Machines (RTM), "Josh, we won the case. The ATM patent is invalid. We are presently preparing our own application with the correct inventor, which is me. Exclusivity of AMT is eliminated and your company can now pursue our bearing system for large rotary tables through my company. I will see to it that all the financial help you provided will be paid back mostly through reduced prices."

Worthington responded, "That is great news Wilson. The fact that the door is now open for RTM to participate in the large table market is enough of a payback. I will instruct our engineers to provide all the necessary information for Tribos to get started on a system for RTM."

Not only did Wilson win the patent infringement case, but he gained another captive customer that would materially increase the business of Tribos. Also, while he was gone, Homer had completed most of the work on the NASA SBIR seal program. The results of the Phase 1 effort looked very good with both the seal configurations and the test rig conceptual designs completed in a high quality manner. What remained was some computer performance predictions, an indication of the tasks for a Phase 2 effort and the final report. Wilson scheduled one month for completion of the Phase 1 effort.

Wilson met with Jim Clairborne to discuss important matters for Tribos Engineering. With the increased work load, Wilson felt that the company would need three more engineers, two more technicians and two more designers experienced with the computer design program that Tribos was using. Also, Jim indicated that his marketing effort had led to additional opportunities for porous bearings for Air Cycle Machines and Turbochargers. Wilson agreed to investigate these opportunities further with Jim.

HELIUM BUFFER SEAL AND NIH

Several months later, Tribos was awarded The Phase 2 Helium Buffer Seal contract. The Phase 2 contract was a proof of concept program. Most of the design and analytical work of the seals were done in Phase 1. It was necessary to complete design of the test rig that was completed in 3 months' time. Manufacture and test was the tasks ahead. Drawings of the belt driven test rig, and the two seal designs was sent out for manufacture. Two seal concepts were being considered. The main element of one seal design was made entirely of carbon. Pressurized air flows though orifice restrictors into the clearance space between the seal ring and the shaft. The air exits from both sides to prevent hydrogen on one side from mixing with oxygen on the other side. A second configuration consisted of a metallic support with an inverted T crossection, with porous compound interfaces. The inside bore has a porous carbon cylindrical interface and the sides of the inverted T have vertical porous carbon interfaces. The porous components are epoxied to their steel supporting structure which contains cutouts to feed supply pressure to the porous interfaces. The porous material interfaces will be impregnated with the C-5 resin until the required pressure drops and flows are satisfied.

Manufacture took several months, but it was soon time to assemble and test. Helium was supplied by a tank truck parked outside with the helium piped into the test area. The tests consisted of steady state, shaft unbalance, shaft misalignment and start stop runs. The carbon seals were first tested and the results were quite good. A 10 percent reduction in helium flow from the presently used seals was noted. The only problem with the carbon seals was some wear at the anti-rotation pin receptacles. The porous carbon seals were exceptional. They operated at lower clearances than the pure carbon seals and the flow levels were extremely low. Every test of the porous carbon seals was successful and over 100 hours of test runs were accumulated without noticeable wear. A final report was issued to NASA, which was very well received. The responsibility for marketing the seals was left to the Tribos Company.

The seal design was meant to fit the envelope of a rocket engine manufactured by the Stage 1, Company of Los Angeles California. Wilson wanted to convince Stage 1 management to employ porous seals on their rocket engines. Wilson prepared an extensive Power Point presentation. He and Jim Clairborne made the trip to California.

A sizeable audience of engineers witnessed the presentation. Wilson explained the advantages of the porous carbon seals and thoroughly detailed the design configuration, the test procedures and the test results. The audience seemed interested but aloof. Afterwards, Wilson met with Stage 1 management to determine their interest in incorporating the porous seals into their machinery. Their management said that it would be too difficult to incorporate new seals into their engines even though the seal design was interchangeable with their present face seals. Wilson explained that the helium savings of the Tribos seals would allow significant increase in satellite payload. That did not phase Stage 1 management one iota. They made additional lame excuses why they could not use the seals. They thanked Wilson and Jim for coming and bid them farewell.

Over dinner that evening, Wilson asked Jim, "What happened today? I thought that Stage 1 would be overjoyed with our seal. Instead they sloughed us off as a bunch of hacks." Jim replied, "Wilson, you witnessed a typical case of NIH syndrome." Wilson seemed perplexed, "The only NIH that I know is The National Institute of Health. What do they have to do with anything?" Jim laughed and responded, "In this case NIH stands for Not Invented Here. I have encountered it several times. If the idea does not emanate from their organization, they will have nothing to do with it even though it would have decided advantages. They put up a brick wall to any outside influence. Today we witnessed a perfect example." Wilson conjectured, "There must be applications that could use our seal. We have to research for potential applications, and I want to patent the porous carbon seal."

Several days later, Jim met with Wilson at home base. "Wilson, I have found applications for the buffer seal, only it is not used as a buffer seal but as an exclusion seal. It can be used to prevent product loss or contamination. There are numerous opportunities in Oil and Gas, Chemical Processing, Pulp and Paper and Mining among others." Wilson immediately grasped the opportunities. "Good work Jim. We have to hire a Marketing Engineer to seek out business. He must become familiar with the seal, test results, etc. We can tailor the design to the application at hand. How are we doing with the patent?" Jim replied, "That is moving well. The power point presentation supplied a good deal of information for the patent and it is well underway. Perhaps some additional design details will be necessary." Wilson commented, "Good work Jim, perhaps we will be in the seal business."

DREAM, DREAM, DREAM

Things were definitely looking up for Tribos Engineering and Wilson couldn't be happier. Success made him work harder and 12 hour days were common. Soon after, the dreams began. The Guru appeared in Wilsons dreams.

Guru: "Hello Wilson, I am the invention Guru and I will help you with the Oil-Free Piston Engine."

Wilson: "How are you going to help me?"

Guru: Let's consider how to make the piston Oil-Free. Use the pressure built up during the compression stroke to feed a hydrostatic bearing surrounding the piston to accept the side loads imposed by the connecting rod. The bearing should be made of high temperature porous carbon, which provides the hydrostatic restriction. A plenum behind the bearing communicates with the combustion chamber and contains high pressure gas that feeds the porous carbon. Clearance between the piston and carbon is formed by the compression of the carbon. At the top of the piston incorporate a sectored piston ring with a hydrostatic tapered land geometry at the cylinder wall interface. Downstream of the piston ring, vent the flow that escapes through the ring clearance.

Wilson: "Wait a minute, I have lots of questions."

Guru: "Sorry Wilson, work out a design based upon what I have told you. Good night!"

Wilson slept uneasily the rest of the night as he wrestled, in his mind, with the concept that the Guru described.

The next day, at work, Wilson started to sketch a piston as per the Guru's recommendations. When the sketch was completed, he began to understand that the ideas may have merit. He called upon his ace designer, Homer Jennings.

"Homer, I am considering the development of an Oil-Free piston engine. I want to start out with the design of the piston. Here is a pencil sketch of what I have in mind." The two men discussed the piston concept for over an hour. Then, Wilson added, "Homer select a diesel engine we can work with and modify for an Oil-Free evaluation. See if you can obtain the engine's maintenance manual, which might have dimensions we can use. Then layout a piston design, as per our discussion, that fits the engine. Also, delegate whatever other work you are doing. I want you full time on this project. I will have Jim Clairborne set up a work order number for you."

The next night the Guru returned in Wilson's dream. "Now that we have the piston underway, the crankshaft bearings are next. You will need a source of external air pressure to supply each bearing at an inlet groove such that hydrodynamic rotation of the crankshaft will cause the pressure to increase and carry the loads imposed. It is suggested that the source of the supply pressure come from a device that is Oil-Free. Good Luck my friend."

The Guru dreams continued night after night until he had the whole engine on air bearings and completely devoid of oil. Every morning Wilson would make a sketch of the Gurus suggestions. He set up a notebook to insert all the sketches that he made. Every part of the engine that was lubricated with oil was covered including the two mentioned above (piston skirt and crankshaft), piston wrist pin, the camshaft and camshaft bearings, the connecting rod and its bearings. The notebook became quite full. He discussed each application with Homer who assiduously studied the concepts until they were engrained in his head. He would also sketch each concept, but dimensional drawings would have to wait until an actual engine was selected.

There were three forms of lubrication being applied to the engine. They were:

Hydrodynamic –Due to rotation that drags the lubricant into a converging wedge that builds up fluid pressure.

Hydrostatic – A source of external pressure is introduced into the film providing load capacity.

Squeeze film –When two surfaces separated by a lubricant are closed towards each other pressure buildup occurs in the film.

For the Oil-Free engine, the piston is lubricated by a combination of hydrostatic and squeeze film.

The crank shaft bearings are lubricated by a combination of hydrostatic and hydrodynamic.

The wrist pin is lubricated by squeeze film

The cam shaft is lubricated by a combination of hydrodynamic and hydrostatic.

The connecting rod is lubricated by a combination of hydrodynamic and squeeze film.

ORGANIZATION

Wilson called Jim Clairborne into his office. "We are going to have to do something with the way we are organized. In the beginning, I could handle many of the engineering chores, but the company has grown beyond my capabilities. We have to delegate more responsibilities. We need a project leader for the ATM contract, and a project leader for the RTM project, and we need a project leader for new business activities such as turbochargers and air cycle machines. Also, we need a project leader for seals. I want to stick to porous carbon externally pressurized air bearings and seals in all cases, and I believe we should have someone that can improve on our design codes and develop advanced analytical tools. I want to relieve myself of many of these duties, because I am interested in developing an Oil-Free piston engine and I want to dedicate myself to that task. Would you agree with my assessment on organizational changes?" Clairborne replied, "Absolutely! I have been thinking about this for some time and I am glad you bought it up. Several engineers from our previous employment at Mechanical Analytics are unhappy with their new employment and I am sure they would be willing to join us. As a matter of fact several have approached me already. Although, we have a pretty steady income from our existing projects, funding could be a problem. To be reasonably comfortable, we should have additional funds to call upon. I suggest we try to get a line of credit from the TriCities bank. We are going to have to put the company up as collateral." Wilson thought about what Jim said, but he understood the situation. Wilson was well aware of the need for additional capital. "All right Jim. Do you want me to go to the bank with you?" Clairborne answered, "No Wilson. I think I can handle it. I will try to arrange a Five Hundred Thousand dollar line of credit. Of course, you will have to sign loan papers." Wilson responded, "OK Jim. Go to it, and thanks for your efforts. With regards to the delegated projects I want to arrange a review schedule with the principal personnel so that I am kept abreast of progress, problems, etc. One other thing Jim. We should be looking for an electrical engineer who could help us develop a resonant piston compressor, which I am considering to be a component of an Oil-Free piston engine."

During the next several weeks, Jim Clairborne was able to procure a line of credit from the bank. Both he and Wilson were able to interview and hire three more engineers. The company was beginning to shape up as a real enterprise.

THE DIESEL

Wilson met with Homer to review the Oil-Free progress. Homer had picked out a 500 horse power 6 cylinder in line diesel and had been able to purchase a maintenance manual. The piston diameter was 4 inches. He had begun to lay out a piston design when Wilson called. "I have some more information Homer regarding the crankshaft bearings. Each bearing is to have an inlet groove where a source of external pressure is to be injected. Then, hydrodynamic action will increase the pressure as the air flows into a converging wedge due to rotation. A second alternative is a porous carbon hybrid bearing that develops pressure by a source of external pressure and by hydrodynamic action due to rotation. I have made pencil sketches of both types for you to consider in the design process."

The entire engine was lubricated with pressurized air. The piston itself used the pressurized air due to the compression stroke while the other components used external air pressure. The missing piece was the source of external pressure.

Besides working on the Oil-Free engine, mostly with Homer, Wilson had to keep abreast of the other projects the company was engaged in. Tribos had received a major contract from a turbocharger manufacturer to apply air bearings to their system. It soon became apparent to Wilson that since he no longer could be intimately engaged with every project an extensive education process was required. He met regularly with each project engineer and provided as much individual instruction as possible. A project engineer would be responsible for analysis and overseeing design, production, test and reporting. Over time, Wilson could see that progress was being made and the engineering staff was catching on. Wilson was adamant that each project be done efficiently and properly and that the reputation of Tribos Engineering be maintained at a high level. Jim Clairborne undertook marketing activities and proposal preparation, and was indispensable to the organization. As time progressed and the company advanced additional personnel were added as required and an appropriate organization chart developed. In the interim, Wilson did his best to concentrate on the Oil-Free engine.

RESONANT PISTON COMPRESSOR

Joshua Bentley was the electrical engineer hired by Jim Clairborne, and he met with Wilson to discuss the application of a resonant piston compressor. A resonant piston compressor contains a spring mass system that has a natural frequency in the vibration mode. If the system can be designed to operate at its natural frequency, then very little energy is required to vibrate the compressor. In addition to Joshua, Wilson called Edgar Neuman, a design engineer to the meeting.

Wilson proceeded, "As you probably know, we are trying to develop an Oil-Free piston engine. A major requirement is a source of external air pressure. If a resonant piston compressor is feasible, then the energy required to drive the compressor can be significantly reduced. I have made some pencil sketches of possible configurations. I was thinking about an opposed piston arrangement with piston diameters of 3 or 4 inches. I want you to research these configurations and others that come to mind in order to produce the pressure and flow that I have estimated will be needed. From the mass and spring support, the vibration natural frequency can be established. Determine if the opposed piston arrangement can be driven at the natural frequency and provide the necessary mass flow and pressure. Are there any questions?" Wilson was glad that both Joshua and Edgar had a multitude of questions, and he liked their enthusiasm concerning the assigned project. The meeting took most of the day, and Wilson felt confident that Joshua and Edgar would come up with a workable concept.

HARDWARE

The design phase of the Oil-Free project was proceeding quite well and Wilson was pleased with the project. Homer had delegated design personnel to complete many of the manufacturing details and it soon became time to manufacture components. The diesel engine selected by Homer was purchased and a top technician named Robert Carpone was assigned to the project. The engine would have to be dismantled and modified to accommodate the new pistons and changes to the crankshaft bearings and the other relevant components. Carpone was very careful and took stock of all bolt torques and other significant dimensions so that the engine would get back together properly. Carpone was a burly gentleman with a height of six feet four and a muscular weight of two hundred fifty pounds. He was a likeable sort with a continuous smile. Wilson was quite impressed with him because he was knowledgeable and intelligent and he felt very confident in his abilities. To accommodate the new piston design, the cylinder bore would have to be increased. Carpone dismantled the head and cylinder block and transported them to the machine shop being used by Tribos. He oversaw the operation and made sure that the bores were machined correctly and witnessed the measurements taken after the operation. The bores were true and within the design tolerances. Carpone then carefully returned the components to Tribos.

As time marched on the Oil-Free diesel was progressing well. The missing piece was the external air supply. At a meeting with Joshua Bentley and Edgar Neuman, Wilson was pleased with the design they had come up with. Calculations indicated that they had met the pressure and flow requirements. However, Joshua indicated that there was difficulty in obtaining resonant operation. Wilson reflected "I think you are close enough to resonance to proceed to manufacture. I do not want to hold up the program to obtain an ideal solution. Therefore, complete the design as presented and then proceed to manufacture. I commend the both of you for an excellent analytical and design job. It is important that we do not lose any of the calculations, sketches etc. as the alternating piston compressors could be a separate product line that we could develop in the future. Joshua, I would like you to coordinate with Julius Workman, our computer expert and proceed to develop computer codes for analyzing the compressor. I will also meet with him as time permits."

The remainder of all parts were in and Wilson wanted to begin testing. Until the compressor was ready, pressurized nitrogen bottles would substitute for external air. The first series of test would be without combustion and the engine would be driven by an electric motor. The purpose of the non-combustion tests was to determine if the pistons would operate with clearance and if the other components such as the crankshaft bearings operated properly.

INITIAL TESTING

Wilson assigned Robert Carpone the responsibility of installing the test setup. He had help from several other technicians and they completed the setup in about three days. The time had come to begin the testing. Nitrogen at 200 pounds pressure was supplied to the engine. Before electric motor drive rotation was activated, the engine was to be rotated by hand. If components were floated as designed, the manual hand rotation should be able to be accomplished without difficulty. Carpone cranked the engine and the rotation was smooth without noticeable drag. Next the motor was connected and the engine was run at motor speed of 3600 revolutions per minute for 30 minutes. Then, the test was stopped and the engine was disassembled for inspection. The crankshaft bearings were fine, but the pistons showed slight rubbing marks and transfer of porous carbon to the pistons. Wilson considered any rubbing to be unacceptable and some design changes had to be made. That evening Wilson considered the options to correct the rubbing problem.

The next morning, Wilson called a meeting with Homer Jennings and Robert Carpone. The cause of the cylinder rubbing problem is insufficient clearance between the porous carbon and the piston due to the fact that the carbon is not compressing enough under pressure. "There are two ways to solve the problem. The thickness of the carbon can be increased or a softer carbon can be applied. Increasing the thickness of the carbon would require increasing the bore of the cylinders, which would be a major job. I have studied some carbon catalogs and found a high temperature carbon with a Modulus of Elasticity considerably less than the one we are using now. If we can use that carbon, there will be no dimensional changes to contend with. The company that makes that carbon has a local representative in the area and I will contact him immediately following this meeting. There is one other design change I want to make. At the top of the cylinder near the combustion chamber we should install a solid ceramic ring. It should reside above the piston ring and have a liberal clearance. The ceramic ring can act as an insulator against the high temperature of combustion. I am not sure the carbon can take those temperatures. Homer make sure the design drawings reflect the dimensional and material changes. Robert see that the carbons that are now used are disassembled and the new ones are properly impregnated with the C-5 resin and then installed in the engine. Also, install the ceramic rings as I described."

It took two months to incorporate the changes to the engine and prepare for another cold test. Both the testing and the inspection went smoothly. There was no evidence of piston-cylinder rubbing and the preliminary cold testing was completed successfully.

REDUCTION TO PRACTICE.

Joshua Bentley and Edgar Neuman had been working diligently on the resonant piston compressor project and it had reached the stage of initial testing. A test arrangement had been set up so that the discharge from the compressor would proceed through a restrictor valve. Both flow and pressure measurements would be taken as well as the power levels required to drive it. The setup and testing occupied most of the day. The results of the testing indicated that pressure and flow requirements could be satisfied, but resonance was not achievable. The power levels to drive the compressor however, were not beyond a pre-defined limit and thus the compressor was acceptable for use.

All the pieces were in place for the full blown hot test. A test plan had been completed. Initially the engine was to be run through a speed range for four hours just to make sure that the Oil-Free engine could work. Subsequently, a full inspection would take place. If the inspection was positive, dynamometer testing would proceed. The complete test program would run for 14 work days. The engine exhaust was directed outside the plant via piping and ducting. The piston compressors were connected to ducting to supply air pressure to a tank whose discharge was directed to the engine. Separate lines were installed between the tank reservoir and the crankshaft and cam shaft. The wrist pins were fed via the cam shaft and the connecting rod bearings were fed via the crankshaft. The setup took several hours. Then the piston compressor, which ran off the engine battery, was energized and the engine was put in "float mode". The engine started smoothly and idled in a quiet manner. The idling continued for about one half hour without signs of distress. Then, the speed was changed in increments of 100 rpm. At each increment the engine maintained speed for about a half hour or so. In addition to the engine purring along, the piston compressor also kept producing the pressurized air without difficulty. Wilson did think to himself that it would be necessary to duplicate the compressor in an actual application since failure of the compressor meant seizure of the engine. Also, speed of the compressor would have to be adjusted to the pressure in the supply tank which was to remain at a constant 200 pounds per square inch regardless of engine speed or load. Also, a bypass blow off would be necessary if pressure became excessive. There definitely was some control engineering required. The four hour initial run was completed without incident and disassembly showed no visible effects. It suddenly dawned on Wilson "We have an Oil-Free engine", and tears swelled in his eyes. This was a very emotional moment for Wilson who believed for many years that an Oil-

Free engine was a distinct possibility. There was still much work to do to complete the test program and incorporate some necessary control changes, but Wilson was very confident of ultimate success. Wilson remarked to Jim Clairborne "This calls for a celebration. Tomorrow at noon have the entire staff congregate in the test area and let's provide snack food and champagne. This is a momentous event. Also, let's assign our best engineer to the project as I will be busy with patents and publicity."

The next day at noon everyone congregated in the diesel engine test area. Wilson opened the festivities with a speech. *"Thank you all for coming. We are here to celebrate a demonstration that took place yesterday of an Oil-Free engine. We still have a long way to go, but yesterday we displayed feasibility. Our company is founded on the principle of innovation. We started out with the floating piston concept for large rotary table support. Porous air bearings have been a mainstay in almost all of our inventions and we are finding applications for turbochargers, air-cycle machines, rotary air compressors and exclusion seals. In addition to the Oil-Free engine we have developed an air bearing piston compressor that feeds the engine. I congratulate all of you for your hard work and diligence and remember, no matter what your job is, think innovation because our future depends on it. Now enjoy yourself for a couple of hours while we celebrate the birth of an Oil-Free engine."*

After returning to his office, Wilson called the patent attorney, Jeremy Patterson.

PATENTS

Wilson had invited Jeremy Patterson over to the plant to witness the Oil-Free engine as it proceeded through the test program. "Jeremy, we have to get started with patents for the Oil-Free engine. I think we should have a patent for every component including the piston and cylinder, the crankshaft bearings, the wrist pin, the connecting rod and the cam shaft. Also, we want to patent the Oil-Free piston compressor that feeds the engine. We have an awful lot of work to do. I have made extensive notes and sketches about every component and of course we have manufacturing drawings, all of which can be made available to you." Jeremy replied, "Very good and congratulations on your success. To expedite the patent process, personal coordination is most helpful. Therefore, a considerable amount of your time will be required." Wilson conjectured, "Let me give that some thought. I did want to be intimately involved in the remainder of the testing and then in the subsequent marketing necessary to obtain contracts. Tell you what Jeremy, I will spend mornings in your office working on the patent applications and afternoons here in the lab."

For the next several months, Wilson worked as he had suggested. The lab results of the engine testing were satisfactory. Torque and horsepower levels, as indicated by dynamometer testing, were slightly better than the published results of the oil counterpart and a 5 percent improvement in fuel consumption was less than the hoped for 10 percent, but nevertheless a welcome statistic. The patent applications were proceeding well and the last application was about a week away. There were several items in Wilson's mind that needed attention.

He asked to meet with his analytical engineer Julian Walker. "Julian, we have had some good initial success, but our engineering efforts have been mostly cut and try and empirical in nature. We have to do better than that. I know you have done a lot of work with the porous bearings and your computer codes have been very helpful. Now we have much bigger things to contend with. I have made a listing of codes that can help us in the design process. These include:

- Kinematic analysis to establish piston and bearing loads.
- Piston analysis to ensure design operating clearance
- Analysis of the piston ring itself to determine clearance and flow
- Crankshaft bearing analysis
- Connecting Rod bearing analysis
- Wrist pin analysis
- Camshaft analysis

- Piston compressor analysis

I know that it will take some time to generate all the codes that are needed and you will need a staff to accomplish these requirements. I anticipate that we will generate substantial research business when we publicize the Oil-Free engine and then we can hire an appropriate staff. In the meantime I have generated a significant amount of analytical notes that you can study and begin to formulate in your mind on how to proceed." Julian appreciated the discussion and appeared anxious to expand his horizons. Wilson concluded "Keep me advised on your progress and requirements."

MARKETING

Wilson and Jim Clairborne discussed the status of the Oil-Free engine program. Wilson began "Jim, we have an Oil-Free diesel engine with demonstrated success. Now is the time to start capitalizing. I am a little concerned that we do not have patents in place, but I am willing to go with "patent pending". Jim replied, "I agree. Although, we have made great strides, our success has not generated income and we are beginning to feel the pinch. We could use additional funding. I would like to avoid going to the bank again." "Ok Jim, that funding gremlin hits us in the face again. We not only need money to pay our present bills, but we need it for expansion purposes including equipment and personnel. Let's lay out a marketing plan to be implemented by you and me. I am not yet willing to give away trade secrets, so we should not discuss design details but proceed in generalities. We certainly do not want to give away our piston configuration until the patents are finalized. Let me give you an outline of the plan I have in mind.

- First, let's develop a Power Point Presentation.
  o Air pressure replaces oil
  o Piston uses pressure of compression
  o Crankshaft, connecting rod, cam shaft uses external pressure.

- External air supplied by oil less piston compressor
- Photo of our diesel arrangement with appropriate call outs
- Performance info
- Patent pending on all components.

- I will work on the power point presentation
- Notify local newspaper, and national media, of our Oil-Free engine
- Contact Department of Energy and request that we give a presentation
- Contact Department of Defense for possible tank engines. Request presentation
- Contact Diesel manufacturers, Request presentation
- Jim, please do most of the contacting.
- Prepare for many presentations and travel. We want to blitz the world.
- We probably will need additional funding before we realize additional contracts. Advise the bank of our discoveries and extend our credit line.

I am visualizing an awful lot of work to do." Jim replied, "I will get started immediately. The plan sounds great."

That evening, Wilson worked on a Power Point Presentation using his computer at home. He tried to use as much pictorial slides as possible as too many word slides defuses an audience. Considering that one objective was to avoid design details until the patents were finalized, the presentation was quite good.

The next day Jim contacted the local newspaper. A reporter and photographer came over to the plant and Jim explained the workings of the engine and permitted distant photographs. He presented the reporter with a copy of the Power Point presentation, which the reporter could use in his article. Jim also sent copies of the power point presentation to technical magazines that liked to present inventive applications. Meanwhile, Wilson made phone calls to government agencies and requested the opportunity to make a presentation. A full-fledged marketing campaign had begun.

Several days later, the newspaper article was published and it aroused significant activity. Wilson was asked to appear before two heavily watched TV talk shows to discuss the engine and what it could mean to the future. Wilson had developed a standard speech. *"To obtain an Oil-Free engine we are replacing oil with pressurized air. The piston is lubricated by the compressed air that the piston develops during the compression stroke. The other engine components, such as the crankshaft bearings and can shaft, are lubricated by air from an external source. Our efforts have been concentrated on a 500 HP diesel engine. We have developed an Oil-Free piston compressor as the external source. Our measurements indicate slightly better power levels than the oil counterpart and fuel efficiency savings of 5 percent. At the present time we are not divulging design details. We have patents pending on all components and the designs will remain proprietary until the patents are awarded."*

Wilson also prepared for the many questions that would come his way. The one he received the most was. "Will the technology be used for automobile engines?" His stock answer, "For use in automobile engines, everything must be miniaturized. That will take some time. Right now our concentration is on large diesel engines that may be used for emergency and auxiliary power and for ship and train propulsion, etc. Before we get to the automobile, we probably will consider heavy truck engines." Generally, his interviews were well received and the publicity was helpful for business promotion.

Jim Clairborne and Wilson made several trips to interested parties. They visited the Department of Energy who had a general interest for efficiency and savings of oil consumption. The Department of the Army had interest for battle tank usage as the avoidance of oil removed a source of vulnerability. Perhaps the most interesting inquiry came from

The Major Electric Company a big conglomerate. One of the subsidiaries of Major Electric made Diesel Electric Locomotives. They invited Tribos to make a presentation. Wilson and Jim traveled to Shoreline, PA on the shores of Lake Erie to present at the Major Electric locomotive facility. The Major Electric personnel were keenly interested in what was presented, but they had some serious questions. Matt Shaughnessy, one of the supervisors at the plant was liaison with Wilson and he queried, "We are dealing with engines of four to five thousand horsepower. Can your system handle that level of power?" Wilson replied, "The horse power levels are not the limiting factor. I am pretty sure we can handle it. Everything must be sized upward accordingly, and the air pressure levels will probably need to be increased from 200 to 400 pounds per square inch. The exact pressure levels will be determined through our proprietary analytical computer codes. It is important however that we know all the geometry of the engine. It probably behooves us to work with the engine manufacturer, but we must safeguard our proprietary designs. As I mentioned before, we have patents pending. We will be able to exchange information in more detail once the patents are issued. Non-disclosure agreements can keep us contractually bonded." Matt replied, "We prefer that you work with us directly rather than the diesel manufacturer. We have all the details of the engine that we can supply to you. We will require however, that you restrict your locomotive activity to Major Electric exclusively." Wilson replied, "That sounds OK. I am sure that we can come to a satisfactory arrangement."

Afterwards Matt escorted Wilson and Jim on a tour of a typical locomotive. The cab area was where the engineers who drive the train reside. Behind them was a mass of complicated machinery with very little space for humans to maneuver. Besides the diesel engine there was an alternator to generate electricity, air intakes for the engine, a rectifier to convert the AC from the alternator to DC for the traction motors on each wheel. There is space for electronic controls a motor blower, driven off the engine, to provide cooling flow to the traction motors, a turbocharger for the engine, an air compressor for providing air for the train brakes and other auxiliary equipment. Wilson commented, "We have our work cut out for us. We are going to have to find space for our piston compressors that feeds the engine. We will need layout drawings of the locomotive components so that we can fit our compressor into an appropriate space." Matt was quite agreeable and requested that Tribos submit a proposal outlining the tasks and costs involved in producing an Oil-Free engine for locomotive use. Wilson replied, "I think the first order of business would be, for both of us, to sign a non-disclosure agreement. In order for us to bid we will need quite a lot of information from Major Electric including, for example, engine drawings " Matt responded, "Please send us your non-disclosure agreement, so that we can start the process."

On the way home, Wilson and Jim discussed The Major Electric situation. "Jim, I want to get in touch with our patent attorney, Jeremy Patterson, to determine if he is willing to draft a non-disclosure agreement and also if he could be involved in drafting a contract. I trust him to safeguard our interests." Jim responded, "Sounds good to me. He is very easy to work with and very competent." Wilson continued, "Jim, I want you to handle all contract and administrative matters. I need to figure out what will be technically necessary to engage in a big contract that I envision with Major Electric. We will need a large space to install their engine. I think we should rent the empty warehouse space adjacent to our plant. I believe that besides Major Electric additional contracts could be forthcoming. The army seemed very interested for an Oil-Free battle tank engine. We will probably have to consider additional personnel. We are getting to the point where a more sophisticated organization will be required. As far as funding goes, we have to require advanced funding from potential customers. I prefer not to go to the bank again, although that might be necessary. We might also consider going public although I believe that to be downstream. Our immediate requirement is to have our patent applications issued."

The following day, Wilson placed a call to Jeremy Patterson, "Jeremy, since we publicized our Oil-Free achievements, we have had significant activity. We have had proposal requests from Major Electric and the Department of the Army. We do need legal expertise, which I am hoping you can provide. A non-disclosure agreement would protect proprietary information of both parties and any contracts that ensue should have legal review. Can you help us?" Jeremy replied, "As you know Wilson, I am a patent attorney and patent work would have to come first, but I think I could find the time to help Tribos. Let's give it a try, but if the patent activity gets too much I will let you know. By the way, I do have some good news for you. Our applications have been accepted by the patent office and all patents have been issued. I believe there were ten in all." When he heard the news, Wilson was ecstatic and he had a hard time containing his pleasure. He wanted to scream out, but he held his decorum. "That's wonderful news, Jeremy. Thank you so much for the assistance you provided in preparing the applications."

Jeremy responded, "Wilson, your descriptive material was wonderfully presented and I am sure that is why the patent office was able to quickly turn the applications around." Wilson retorted, "This is a great day Jeremy. Jim Clairborne will be in touch with you regarding the other items we discussed."

After several weeks all the legal documents between Tribos and Major Electric were signed sealed and delivered. Proposal preparation had been in full swing for two primary customers, Major Electric and The Department of the Army. The proposals were similar although the dollar values were quite different mainly due to the size of each machine. The Major Electric diesel engine was much greater. An outline of tasks was as follows:

- Prepare space for testing
- Install engine
- Disassemble engine
- Modify components as required
- Reassemble engine
- Conduct motor driven tests
- Inspect components
- Install dynamometer
- Conduct engine testing and inspection
- Submit bi-monthly and final reports.

The estimated cost of the Major Electric effort was five million dollars and for the Department of the Army, the cost was five hundred thousand dollars. Neither proposal was a fixed price since it could be difficult to predict unknown circumstances. The work was to be done on a best efforts basis, to stay within the budgeted amount. Also, Tribos required a twenty percent advanced payment from both potential customers. Wilson needed those funds for startup activity, and he felt that the patent position allowed for such a requirement. As far as the schedules were concerned, the Major Electric contract would take twenty four months and the Department of the Army contract was estimated to take eighteen months.

In the interim period between proposal and contract, Jim Clairborne and Wilson met frequently to plan for what was ahead. Wilson conjectured, "We will need lots of space for the Major Electric engine program. I do not want to dismantle our 500 horsepower demo as it provides us with an excellent marketing tool. How are we doing with that empty warehouse space next door?" Jim replied, "It is all set up. All we have to do is sign the lease and pay the first month's rent." Wilson retorted, "OK. Let's go ahead with that and get the space cleaned up and ready to receive the monster diesel. Bob Carpone should supervise that activity. We will also have to make provisions to exhaust outside the building. If the Army job comes through, we can use our present storage room in the rear of our building. The next item is staffing. We probably will need two more engineers and two more technicians." Jim said, "I have several people in mind, but I think we should wait for the advance funds to come in. We are getting a little tight again." Wilson remarked, "The money gremlin again. Perhaps we should consider an Initial Stock Offering (IPO) to increase our cash inventory." Jim replied, "I will look into it. Incidentally, Wilson, we have had several inquiries from diesel manufacturers." Wilson replied, "We will have to put that on hold for a while. We are up to our necks right now with the army and Major Electric."

Two weeks later both contracts were consummated and Tribos Engineering was on a growth path again.

VENTURE CAPITOL

Jefferson Cooper was a junior partner of the Venture Capital firm Inventive Ventures. One of his jobs was to keep a lookout for promising fledgling organizations who might need capital to grow. He often researched recently issued patents for promising applications. The recent patents of Tribos Engineering immediately attracted him. Jefferson studied the patents, which he obtained from the patent office, and was extremely impressed. He said to himself "This technology is a winner. We should invest in this company pronto and get in before others do." Jefferson's older brother Angus Cooper owned the company and was the real power behind it.

Every other week, the hierarchy of the company met to present possible investment opportunities. It was at one of these meetings that Jefferson presented his advocacy for investing in Tribos Engineering. "I have found a company that has developed an Oil-Free diesel engine. The name of the company is Tribos Engineering. They have demonstrated the technology through a 500 horsepower diesel that is situated in their plant. They have amassed ten patents on the engine and its components and the company owns some 15 patents altogether. The company also produces air bearing support for large rotary tables that has garnered widespread use because it avoids the pitfalls of stick-slip found with oil systems and it permits high speed operation without difficulty. As part of the Oil-Free diesel system, Tribos has developed an Oil-Free piston compressor supported by air bearings. The company is extremely innovative, and in my opinion, destined for great things. We can get in on the ground floor by investing in this company." Angus showed keen interest in the presentation and asked, "Jefferson, do you have any idea of the patent worth?" Jefferson replied. "No. I really haven't investigated that aspect, however I would suspect that the patents are worth at least fifty million dollars." Angus then suggested, "Jefferson, do some more investigating and find out the patent worth. Determine what price diesel manufacturers would be willing to pay for patent ownership."

Later that day Jefferson confronted Angus privately in his office. "Angus, why are you so interested in the value of Tribos Engineering patents? The company is a good investment and should reap rewards for us down the road." Angus replied, "That's the trouble Jefferson, down the road could mean years. We have made some bad investments lately and we need to recoup with a quick profit. Let's buy control of Tribos Engineering, dissolve the company and then sell the patents. We could probably make a good quick buck." Jefferson was aghast at what Angus had just said, "Angus, I do not want any part of ruining a good company, so you could make a quick buck. I am out of here." Jefferson slammed the door on his way out. Angus was quite upset with his younger brother, but he was determined to proceed with his plans. He called Jonus Wales into his office. Jonus had a reputation for making a quick kill and was successful in bringing money into the company. He was heavy set and overweight as he was a big lunch eater and drinker. Angus proceeded, "Jonus I want you to take over the Tribos situation and determine the patent worth of the company. Jefferson lost interest in proceeding along those lines. You heard his presentation at the meeting this morning. Here are copies of the patents that Jefferson gave to me. Determine the interest of diesel manufacturers and how much they would be willing to pay for patent ownership on an exclusive basis." Jonus quickly sized up the situation and a knowing glee appeared in his eyes. He remarked to Angus, "I will be happy to do what you ask. I smell a quick profit possibility."

For the remainder of the afternoon and into part of the night Jonus assiduously studied the patents. He did so for several days until he became intimately familiar with the patent details. He then began to investigate various diesel manufacturers. From his research, Jonus decided on large engines as being most adaptable to the Tribos technology. He had to carefully consider his approach to these manufacturers. He considered proposing the following:

My company, Inventive Capital is representing Tribos Engineering for the sale of exclusive rights to their patents. These include rights to their Oil-Free engine technology and rights to their Rotary Table technology. These patent rights will be sold to interested parties of each technology. We have been instructed to sell to the highest bidder. Attached is a listing of all patents. Please indicate your highest bid for each collective group designated Oil-Free and Rotary Table. The sale of these patents is a highly confidential matter to Tribos Engineering and any leaks of this information, including to Tribos, will obviate the sale by Tribos Engineering.

This is a clear case of misrepresentation or false pretenses and could result in prison time for Jonus. He decided not to proceed with this approach but instead to propose the following:

My company, Inventive Capital is considering purchasing control of Tribos Engineering. Tribos has a library of very valuable patents. If a sale is consummated by Inventive, then Inventive might be interested in selling exclusive rights to Tribos patents. These include rights to their Oil-Free engine technology and rights to their Rotary Table technology. If Inventive Capital decides to sell patent rights, they will go to the highest bidder. Attached is a listing of all patents. Please indicate your highest bid for each collective group designated Oil-Free and Rotary Table. The sale of these patents is a highly confidential matter and any leaks of this information, including to Tribos, will obviate the sale.

Jonus drafted a letter with the information as indicated above and he sent it to the CEO's of two major diesel manufacturers, Cosmo Diesels and Deland Diesels. The letters were sent out on Inventive Capital stationary to lend credence to the information contained therein. He signed both letters and left his phone number in case personal discussion was desired.

Jonathan Purcell was the CEO of Cosmo Diesels. He wasn't sure how to interpret the letter from Jonus. He called some of his most trusted supervisors into his office. He distributed copies of the letter to the group and after they had digested the contents asked "What do you think about this?" Jacob LeRue expressed his opinion, "I think Inventive Capital wants to buy Tribos and then sell their patents for a quick profit. They are trying to establish a price for the patents. In my opinion, Tribos does not know that Inventive sent out this letter. However, it would be great to obtain those patents. In my opinion, they are probably worth about 20 million." Jonathan pondered what Jacob said and then remarked, "OK, I will respond to Inventive with a 20 million dollar estimate, but we need more than patents. We would also need the expertise of the inventor, Wilson Shindler." Everyone at the meeting agreed.

A like scenario occurred at the other major diesel manufacturer, Deland Diesels. Jonus delivered the information to Angus, "The diesel patents are worth at least twenty million. Perhaps we could get it up to twenty five through competitive bidding, but they also want the expertise of Wilson Shindler." Angus replied, "I am sure that Shindler wouldn't mind some heavy consulting fees thrown his way in addition to a buyout that will net him millions of dollars. Let's offer Shindler some 12 million to start, and if necessary boost to 15 million."

Jonus's initial contact at Tribos was Jim Clairborne. "Mr. Clairborne, my name is Angus Wales. My company Inventive Capital invests in promising enterprises. We have researched your company and are interested in making a sizeable investment because we feel confident that it will reap rewards for Inventive Capital." Jim responded, "What do you have in mind?" Without hesitation, Jonus presented his case. "We are prepared to buy out your company for 12 million dollars. Inventive Capital has an excellent record in growing small businesses into large corporations. I would be glad to show you a record of our successes." Clairborne responded "Put your offer in writing and I will take it up with Wilson Shindler." Jonus responded, "Very Good, I will fax you our offer, this afternoon."

Wilson was extremely busy with the Major Electric and Army contracts. He was considering alternatives to determine a correct piston-cylinder configuration without having to do much machining on the exiting configuration. The large Major Electric diesel was a V-6 machine with a piston diameter of 8 inches. Any configuration mistakes could require very costly remachining.

Jim Clairborne interrupted Wilson with the offer from Inventive. Wilson indicated, "Jim, leave the letter on my desk in the office. I will review it when I get home tonight."

MAUREEN

That evening Wilson returned home around 7:00 PM. He had with him the offer from Inventive Capital. Maureen, had been teaching at her elementary school until 3:00 PM, and she stayed another two hours to mark papers and plan for the next day and for a Parents Teacher Conference scheduled for next week. She had time to make turkey sandwiches with lettuce and tomato and mayonnaise on Kaiser Rolls. The sandwiches and store bought potato salad coupled with canned tomato soup comprised the couple's dinner that night. Wilson liked a supper that was not too heavy and he delighted in the sandwich. Maureen remarked, "Wilson, you look very tired. I think you are over doing it at work and you are a prime candidate for burn out." Wilson replied, "I will try to ease off somewhat, but the Major Electric job is very important to Tribos and I must carefully watch every move. Their diesel engine is a humongous machine and any misstep could be very costly."

After dinner Wilson retired to his easy chair with the intent of reviewing the Inventive proposition. He read a few words and then his head turned downward and his eyes closed. He leaned back and the chair reclined and Wilson fell fast asleep. Maureen cleaned up in the kitchen and put the few dishes from supper in the dishwasher after some quick pre cleaning. Afterwards, she retired to the den where Wilson was sleeping. Maureen noted that the Inventive proposal was on the floor lying next to Wilson's feet. She picked it up and glanced at the words. She was aghast at what she saw. Was Wilson prepared to sell his company after all the effort he had put in to get to a highly successful enterprise? Who was Inventive Capital? What did they know about running an innovative technical organization? She decided to bring up the subject with Wilson when he awakened.

It was less than an hour later that Wilson awakened. The Inventive proposal was on the lamp table next to his recliner. He glanced at it and couldn't fathom the meaning behind the proposition. He decided that he would talk it over with Jim Clairborne in the morning. When he went in to the bedroom, Maureen was still up marking papers at her desk in the bedroom. She commented, "Wilson, while you were sleeping that piece of paper you are carrying fell on the floor. I picked it up and read it. I hope you are not thinking of ceding control of your company after you have slaved for many years building it up. Please be very careful and think hard before you make a disastrous decision." Wilson responded, "I really haven't given it much thought. I suppose that I should feel good about someone willing to pay some 12 million dollars for my company. Cash flow is always a gremlin to contend with. Don't worry yourself about it. I will talk to Jim in the morning." Maureen admonished one last time, "Wilson, do not give up control of your company to strangers who know nothing about your technology." Wilson digested her words and went into the bathroom to brush his teeth and prepare to retire for the night.

The next morning, Wilson called Jim into his office. "Jim, what do you make of this proposition?" Jim responded, "I don't like it very much. I researched Inventive. They are a Venture Capital outfit that invests in so called promising companies. However, over 50 percent of their investments have resulted in failed organizations, and they pick up the assets and sell them for profit. I would not cede control to them." Wilson deliberated for a few minutes, "Offer them 20 percent of the company for 3 million dollars. Under no conditions are they to have control." Jim responded, "Sounds good to me."

About one half hour later Jim Clairborne received a call from Jonus Wales. "Mr. Clairborne, do you have a decision regarding our offer?" Jim responded, "Yes, Mr. Shindler will not cede control. He will sell 20 percent of the company for 3 million dollars." Jonus retorted, "Mr. Clairborne, we must have control. We have access to expert management that could make your organization grow at an accelerated clip.

Please advise Mr. Shindler that we must have control." Jim responded, "Mr. Shindler told me directly that under no circumstances would he cede control. Our counter offer is 20 percent for 3 million dollars." Jonus fidgeted and said, "Hold on for a sec, while I consult management." Jonus had no intention of consulting anyone and he scanned his newspaper for an interim period of 5 minutes. "Mr. Clairborne, we are prepared to up the ante to 15 million, but we must have control." By this time. Jim was very frustrated with Mr. Wales who didn't seem to get the message. Jim slammed down the phone. Tribos never heard from Inventive Capital again.

Two days later, Jim received a call from Jonathan Purcell, the CEO of Cosmos Diesels. "Jim, we are anxious to work with Tribos, so that some of our engines are Oil-Free. The last time we talked you indicated that Tribos was working on an arrangement that might be suitable to both parties." Jim responded, "Jonathan, we are getting closer to putting together a package for you to review. Give us several more weeks. We are looking for a way to supply a piston cylinder configuration that you could install at your factory. We would also supply the crank shaft bearings, piston compressors and instructions for modifying the engine components. Wilson Shindler, the head of our company and the brains behind it has been tied up with some major contracts, but he understands the situation and will get to it as soon as he can. We have been hit very hard with inquiries since our successful launch of our demo engine." Jonathan retorted, "We understand Jim. Just don't forget about us. By the way, we were wondering whether Tribos was still considering the sale of your patents. We did have an inquiry about that." Jim was aghast when he heard what Jonathan just said. "Jonathan, where did you get that idea from. We would never sell our patents that we worked so hard to create." Jonathan responded, "I am sorry Jim. I wasn't supposed to mention anything about the patents. There was this Venture Capital outfit who seemed to be promoting the patent sale. I am glad you are keeping the technology where it belongs. Don't forget about us, and have a good day. Goodbye."

Jim was furious when he heard what Inventive Capital had in mind. They were going to buy Tribos, dismantle the organization and sell the patents for a profit. He quickly contacted Wilson and relayed the information he had just heard.

Wilson was in his office devising plans for the Major Electric contract. When he heard the news that Jim had communicated, he breathed a big sigh of relief. He thought to himself, "There are lots of unscrupulous people out there in the business world. Thank god for Maureen, who saw through the scheme at the outset and admonished me not to cede control. I have to take her out to dinner tonight and thank her mightily for her sound advice."

MAJOR ELECTRIC

The major electric job presented some unique challenges to Wilson. Previously, things were done on an AD-Hoc basis. Everything was accomplished in a linear progression. Nothing was done in parallel. Things had to change in order to complete the Major Electric contract in an efficient manner. Wilson purchased a Project Management computer code that allowed tasks to be defined with duration and assigned personnel. He outlined the tasks as follows:

- Conduct analysis to determine:
    - Cylinder configuration
    - Piston configuration
    - Air pressure and flow requirements
- Complete design drawings of:
    - Cylinder inserts
    - Pistons
    - Piston compressor after determining configuration from Joshua Bentley
- Purchase or rent portable crane to allow removal of heavy components
- Purchase or rent high powered dynamometer to be used for engine testing
- Dismantle engine to allow for configuration changes

- Bore out cylinders to desired dimensions on site
- Install cylinder inserts
- Reassemble engine after all components have been modified
- Connect engine to dynamometer
- Install all instrumentation
- Conduct testing

To initiate the program, Wilson called a meeting of all relevant personnel. The attendees included:

- Julian Walker; Analysis
- Homer Jennings; Design
- Gerry Albertelli; Manufacturing
- Bob Carpone; Technicians
- Frank Klamberg; Testing
- Joshua Bentley; Piston Compressor
- Jim Clairborne, Administration

Wilson began the meeting, "I called you all to discuss the Major Electric project. I consider the project to be the most important we have ever obtained and it bears directly on the future of the company. On the screen I have outlined tasks for a successful completion, which I have generated from a project management computer code. I have also given handouts to each of you if you opt to desk follow. As we move along, I want your honest assessment as to your ability to complete as indicated. Overall, the concept is to manufacture cylinder liners that can be directly installed into the cylinder block, and to modify the other components of the engine to permit Oil-Free operation. We have been given a great deal of information on the present engine, such as cylinder bore, stroke and pressure levels that will enable us to get a good start on the redesign.

The first task is to generate preliminary layouts of the cylinder liners and the piston configuration. We will use the best estimate from the configuration used in the demo engine. We have to contend with an 8 inch diameter piston rather than the 4 inch used on the demo engine. Homer, how do you feel about the preliminary layout?" Homer replied, "I have no trouble with the layout except for the thickness of the carbon. I can only estimate that based on the compression pressures involved."

Wilson, "That would be good enough to start. Joshua should be able to supply appropriate information once his analysis is completed. One other thing, Homer. I want a cold test rig that would allow us to determine whether the piston cylinder configuration is correct. Our experience is that if it works cold then it would work with combustion. The rig should have the same stroke as the engine and the same speed spectrum. We want to simulate the compression stroke pressures. You can use a crankshaft drive or whatever else you deem appropriate."

Homer, "I will give that some thought. I am sure we can come up with something applicable."

Wilson, "Julian, Your analysis is critical. We want to know the supply pressure and flow requirements for the crankshaft and camshaft bearings so that Joshua can begin design of the external piston compressors. Also, because the piston compressor is critical to engine operation, there are to be two compressors installed on the engine. One is a spare in case of malfunction of the main compressor."

Wilson, "Bob Carpone, we will have to disassemble the engine to get at all the parts to be modified. Obtain the tools and rigs you will need to disassemble and reassemble"

Carpone, "OK Wilson. I have started a list of materials already, and I know what crew I will be using."

Wilson, "Frank, look into obtaining a high powered dynamometer and obtaining appropriate instrumentation for in house testing.

Wilson, "Gerry, alert our manufacturing subcontractor of the work ahead. Also tell him, everything must be inspected and we want the inspection reports. The most immediate task is the cold test rig. The bore of the cylinder block must be increased to accommodate the cylinder inserts. It is an extremely heavy piece and too much trouble to ship out. Therefore, we want to bore the cylinders in place. Look into getting a portable boring machine by purchase or rent and try to do so within the allotted schedule. It has to be very accurate. We don't want any crooked bores.", "Gotcha boss. I have the machining requirements in the back of my head and I believe I know where I can get things done."

Wilson, "Today we have had a start on the Major Electric contract. We have had a good meeting and I am confident in your abilities. I am planning progress meetings every other month. Thank you all for coming. Jim, can you stick around for a little while longer?"

Wilson, "Jim, the requirements of the Major Electric diesel and our methodology of handling them has opened up some new opportunities. The idea of installing, a cylinder liner in the engine can be transferred to almost any diesel engine regardless of size. We can manufacture cylinder liners remotely from the engine. We do not need the engine here to make it Oil-Free. If the manufacturer gives us the required information we can analyze, design and manufacture the components needed without the need to have the engine here, and we can instruct the manufacturer to make necessary changes to internal components such as the connecting rods. We will make the cylinder liners, pistons, crankshaft and cam shaft bearings, and provide the piston compressors. This approach could be a substantial money maker. Jonathan Purcell of Cosmo Diesels has been enthusiastically wanting to work with us. Also, Deland has shown keen interest. Let's plan this out and market our wares"

Clairborne, "Sounds great Wilson, I will get on it right away. The biggest factor is price. We must charge a premium because of our patent status."

Wilson strongly agreed.

The meeting took most of the day, but now the wheels were turning to develop a locomotive Oil-Free diesel engine and to initiate a significant business opportunity.

Some 6 months later the plant was buzzing with activity. The cold test rig was completed and the cylinder liners and pistons had been manufactured. The first cold test in the test rig was scheduled for next week. Also, initial contracts were awarded by Cosmo and Deland Diesel companies.

The first test of the Major Electric cylinder liner and piston combination indicated excellent friction characteristics, but the leakage past the piston ring was too high. Changes were made to the piston ring and piston configuration to increase the closing loads on the split piston ring. The leakage was reduced to satisfactory levels and the cylinder liners and piston designs were completed and checked out.

To install the cylinder liners in the engine, the cylinder diameters in the engine had to be increased. A portable boring machine was rented and was to be used for the machining operation. An expert in the use of the portable borers was hired to complete the boring operation of all six cylinders. The setup was the most important and necessary component of the boring operation. A tripod was installed above each cylinder and secured in place. Measurements insured near perfect alignment prior to activating the boring tool. Care was taken to remove all scrap chips produced by the operation. After the boring operation on the 6 cylinders, the cylinder liners containing the porous pressurized piston supports were installed. When the engine head was reinstalled, placement of the piston compressors, that supplied various components of the engine, had to be considered. Because of the space limitations on the locomotive, it was decided to place the compressors on top of the engine. Since the compressors were critical to engine operation, Wilson insisted that two compressors be installed, with one acting as a spare in case the main compressor failed. The time had come for a cold test of the engine.

Matt Shaughnessy, from Major Electric, was the primary liaison with Tribos. He visited Tribos to witness the cold test of the engine and the subsequent hot test to establish feasibility of Oil-Free operation. Tribos did not have the equipment for full load tests and it was agreed that they would be done at the Major Electric locomotive facility where sophisticated test and measuring equipment existed.

The engine had been buttoned up and a large variable speed electric motor was coupled to the drive shaft. The piston compressors were energized and the crank shaft was free floating. The electric motor began turning the engine. The cold test went through a spectrum of speeds without difficulty and operation was as smooth as silk. Matt Shaughnessy was quite impressed. After a 4 hour run, the engine was shut down, and an inspection procedure was initiated. The pistons and cylinder liners were in perfect condition as were the crankshaft bearings. Matt was very impressed so far. The engine was reassembled and fueled up in preparation for a combustion test to be held the next day.

That evening, Wilson invited Matt to dinner at a nearby restaurant. Matt divulged some of Major Electric plans for an Oil-Free engine. "Wilson, we have been talking to Cross Country Railroad and they are keenly interested in an Oil-Free locomotive. Avoiding oil changes and increased efficiency can save them lots of money. We will discuss those plans after the engine meets all of our requirements. Also, if the engine passes, we anticipate initiating a large publicity campaign." Wilson responded, "That sounds great. We will take all the publicity we can get. The more people know what we can do, the more business will be developed."

Matt continued, "If all goes well tomorrow, then ship the engine back to our plant by flatbed truck. We have a sophisticated test stand and data acquisition system that can measure torque-speed performance under steady state and transient conditions, fuel efficiency, etc. I anticipate a week of testing to determine if we can install the engine in a locomotive." Wilson responded, "We will have representation during the testing process. Incidentally, the engine uses a turbocharger with oil bearings. I would recommend that we install porous hydrostatic air bearings in the turbocharger, so that all oil is removed from the locomotive. The air can be supplied from our piston compressors that feeds the engine." Matt thought that was a great idea even if the schedule is moved forward and the cost increases. He gave permission to proceed with turbocharger air bearings."

The following day a hot combustion test was run. Fuel was added to the engine. The starting sequence was first to start the piston compressors and energize all bearings and cylinders. Then the engine was rotated and started by cylinder combustion. The engine ran very smoothly, and the test procedure required operation at varying speeds. The total test would take 8 hours, followed by a rigorous inspection of primary components including cylinders, pistons and bearings.

Everything proceeded as planned and the engine was ready for shipment to Major Electric, except for installation of air bearings in the turbocharger. It would take another month or so to design, build and test the air bearings for the turbocharger. Subsequently, the engine and turbocharger had met all Tribos requirements and the engine was shipped by truck to the Major Electric factory for load testing.

Wilson assigned Bob Carpone and Frank Klamberg to be liaison with Major Electric during their testing program. Bob was familiar with all components of the engine that he had taken apart and reassembled several times. Frank was familiar with all the test work that was conducted at the Tribos facility.

Bob and Frank traveled to Shoreline, PA to visit The Major Electric plant. While they were there, the Oil-Free diesel arrived and it was immediately installed in one of the test beds. The test bed consisted of a room with concrete walls and ceiling, with an explosion proof steel door and viewing window. The entire test would be done remotely, and a multitude of wires and sensors were attached to the engine. The wires were threaded through piping and culminating into an extensive data acquisition system located outside the test cell. The test setup took most of the day and the first series of tests were scheduled for tomorrow. Bob and Frank retired to a nearby hotel.

Meanwhile, back at the Tribos facility, there was plenty of activity. The approach to supplying pistons and cylinder liners in addition to bearings and piston compressors was working out very well for Tribos and the diesel engine prototype business was very busy. Wilson felt very confident about the Major Electric diesel. He expected strong publicity after installation on a locomotive and he was considering how to handle the publicity when it arrived. He called Jim Clairborne into his office to discuss how to handle the publicity. Jim offered his opinion, "I think we should be proactive and reach out to as many media outlets as possible. That can only help our business. I would be happy to work on some press releases that can be applied when the time is ripe." Wilson thought that was an excellent idea and encouraged Jim to proceed.

The first series of tests at Major Electric was about to begin. Bob and Frank anxiously watched the proceedings. The start button was pressed and the piston compressors came alive followed by a combustion start of the engine. The engine came up to idle speed in very smooth fashion indeed. Before load testing was applied the engine was run at varying speeds for 10 minutes duration each. A water brake dynamometer was installed in the test cell and connected to the drive shaft. A wide spectrum of tests followed including:

- Crankshaft torque and angular velocity
- Intake air and fuel consumption rates
- Air-fuel ratio
- Pollutant concentrations in the exhaust gas
- Temperature and gas pressures at several locations on the engine body
- Durability testing over an extended period of time

The entire test program was completed in a period of two weeks. All test results were very encouraging. The engine made power requirements without difficulty and a 10% improvement in fuel efficiency was demonstrated. Bob and Frank were elated and they kept Wilson advised of the results every day. Major Electric made the decision to install the engine on the test locomotive. Bob and Frank returned home.

After the successful testing of the Oil-Free engine and the installation aboard a locomotive the Public Relations department of Major Electric went into full swing. A plan had been conceived that included the Cross Country Railroad. The Oil-Free locomotive was to pull a freight train across country from Portland, Oregon to Philadelphia, Pennsylvania. Advertising of this event included TV, newspapers and magazines.

The annual report to stockholders of the Major Electric Company was to be held in an amphitheater in New Jersey. The event was sold out because of the locomotive advertising. The CEO's of Major Electric, Cross Country Railroad and Tribos Engineering were to make a joint presentation. Wilson Shindler of Tribos was to present the development of the engine while George Nation of Major Electric was to discuss the locomotive application and Chris Conamacki of Cross Country Railroad was to discuss the advantages to freight operation. The presentation was to be broadcast on prime TV and a subsequent press conference was to be held.

At the conference, George Nation made some introductory remarks:

Before we get into our business performance, we want to discuss an exciting venture that Major Electric is involved with. I am sure that most of you are aware that our locomotive division is embarking on some exciting advanced technology, namely an Oil-Free diesel engine to power our locomotives. We have commissioned Tribos Engineering, the inventor of the technology to modify our standard 6 cylinder diesel engine for Oil-Free operation. They have done so and our in plant testing has been very rigorous and positive. We are now ready to field test the Oil-Free locomotive with a cross-country freight delivery. With us today are Wilson

Shindler of Tribos Engineering who will discuss the principles of operation and development details and Chris Conamacki of Cross-Country Railroad who will discuss the benefits of the engine to railroad operation.

It was now Wilson's turn and he used a power point presentation.

The principle of operation for an Oil-Free piston engine is to replace the oil lubricant with pressurized air and that principle is enumerated on the first slide. The components involved requiring major design changes are the pistons, the cylinder liners, the crankshaft bearings and the cam shaft bearings as indicated on slide 2. Slide 3 indicates that the pistons are lubricated by the pressurized air of the compression stroke and the other components by an external pressurized air supply. Slide 4 shows our piston compressor used to supply external pressurized air and the compressors are Oil-Free utilizing air lubricated bearings for support and thrust load. Slide 5 is a photograph of the modified engine at the Tribos facility. The piston compressors are located atop the engine so that they can fit into the allotted space in the locomotive compartment. Slide 6 is a graph showing the power density of the Oil-Free engine in comparison to the conventional engine. The reduced friction of the Oil-Free engine results in a 10 percent increase in power under most operating conditions. The final slide shows that the Oil-Free engine has a 10 percent increase in efficiency which translates to a significant reduction in fuel consumption.

After Wilson's presentation, Chris Conamacki presented the railroads perspective citing economic savings due to less maintenance and better fuel consumption. The numbers were very significant.

George Nation concluded the presentation by stating that a press conference has been scheduled at the conclusion of the stock holder's meeting.

At the press conference, the three principals sat at a table with individual microphones. The TV cameras were on and the broadcast went nationwide on a major network. George Nation, CEO of Major Electric opened the proceedings:

Good afternoon. The subject of this press conference is to answer your questions regarding the Oil-Free locomotive developed in concert with Tribos Engineering. Here at this table is Wilson Shindler, president of Tribos Engineering, and inventor of the Oil-Free components of the engine, and Chris Conamacki, President of Cross Country Railroad. As most of you know, we are engaging in a trial run of the Oil-Free engine, by delivering a freight load from Portland, Oregon to Philadelphia, PA. During our stockholders meeting, Mr. Shindler discussed the principles behind the development of the engine and Chris Conamacki presented the advantages to railroad operation. Please specify who your question is directed to.

Question: Mr. Shindler, your presentation this morning did not show many details of the engine components. Is that information available?

Wilson: It was not appropriate to get into engineering details at the stockholders meeting. We have over twenty patents describing our technology, which are available to the general public.

Question: Mr. Shindler, what is the engine horsepower and how many freight cars will be involved in the cross country run?

Wilson: The engine horsepower is 4000. It is a six cylinder engine. The engine will be pulling some 20 loaded freight cars in addition to a spare locomotive with conventional lubrication. We are looking at bigger engines in the 10,000 to 13,000 horsepower range. We expect a 2 to 3 year development time frame.

The press conference continued for over an hour. A wide audience watched the TV proceedings and there was no one more interested in the program than Mr. Horace Neeley.

SABOTAGE

Along route 147 in New York State an interesting and different sight appears to the vehicle driver. Normality provides a McDonalds and Dunkin Donuts, doctors and veterinarian offices, and a glimpse of the countryside. Then appears a huge black steel fence surrounding a property of some 100 acres with a well-manicured lawn and beautiful flower beds. A gate opens to a road that leads to a system of - coordinated architectural designed structures that make up the home offices of The Neeley Chemical Company. The company is family owned and highly successful in manufacturing additives for lubricants. They have developed a very strong business in diesel engine lubrication, being the only supplier of proprietary additives.

After watching the Major Electric press conference Horace Neeley went into a cold sweat. He felt threatened like never before. Horace was 52 years old and had been running the company for some 5 years. He was a man of average height with a well groomed body, which he nurtured daily at a nearby fitness center. His facial features included a strong jaw and thinning blond hair. In his position as CEO, he answered to family stockholders who were used to successful enterprises. He greatly feared his father Stanislaus Neeley who had built the organization to its present elite status. A reduction in the diesel lubrication business could be devastating to the family and in particular to him. To his mind, the Oil-Free engine must not succeed.

Horace called into his office, Augustas Bolen his primary assistant. Augustas had risen through the ranks of Neeley Chemicals by always doing the bidding of Horace, and never disagreeing. His education was in Finance and he could not contribute any technical expertise to the organization. He kept a close eye on the books and made sure they were always in order, assisted in budget preparation and for financial matters he was a valuable contributor. Augustas was in his mid-forties, was small in stature, thin and his black goatee beard was always well groomed. Horace initiated the conversation, "Augustus, we have a major problem on our hands. I have just witnessed a press conference at the Major Electric annual meeting. They are experimenting with an Oil-Free diesel to propel their locomotives. They have contracted with a company called Tribos Engineering who has developed the Oil-Free engine. We have spent millions developing additives for diesel oil, with great success. That business could go kaput if the Oil-Free engine is successful. An Oil-Free diesel could be disastrous for our company and for me personally." Augustus interjected, "Horace, we have always been able to find alternative applications for our additives. I have confidence we can do so again." Horace continued, "Not so Augustus. The additive was developed solely for diesel engines, and finding another application would be extremely difficult. Major Electric is combining with The Cross Country Railroad for an Oil-Free engine demonstration. I believe the Oil-Free locomotive will pull a freight train across country from Portland Oregon to Philadelphia. We should do everything possible to ensure that the demo is unsuccessful. Do you get what I mean? You can use cash from the slush fund as needed. The demo is scheduled to occur in about a month. I want you to drop everything you are doing and concentrate on ruining the demo's debut. "

Augustus bemoaned the fact that he had a difficult and unpleasant job to perform. He thought to himself, "This comes with the territory. If I want to secure my position with the company, I have to do his bidding. How can I destroy the demo if I know nothing about it? I have to assign an engineer to get me the details."

Augustus called into his office one of the well-reputed engineers, of the company, Jon Schwartz. "Jon, Mr. Neeley has given me an assignment and I need your help. Major Electric is experimenting with an Oil-Free diesel engine, for which our company has considerable interest. The engine has been invented by a company called Tribos Engineering. We are considering investing in that company but we have to know more of the details of the engine. Tribos has accumulated a series of patents about the engine. Since patents are in the public domain, we can study them to find out the engine details. Please review whatever you can find out about the engine and get back to me in a week." Jon replied, "Sounds interesting, but I do have other work that requires my attention." Augustus admonished, "Jon, this is of the highest priority. Please put aside your other work until you have finished this task. Report back in one week."

After one week, Augustus called Jon into his office. "Jon, what have you found out?" Jon replied, "I was able to view the patents on the internet. The creativity by Wilson Shindler was ingenious. Basically, he replaced the oil lubricant by pressurized air. The piston was lubricated by the pressurized air of the compression stroke, and the rest of the engine by external piston compressors. The piston compressors use air bearing support as does the engine turbocharger. They have eliminated oil completely. I don't understand all of the details, but that summarizes the inventions. I also managed to obtain a magazine article about the engine for Major Electric's locomotive engine. The engine utilizes most of the available space so the piston compressors are mounted on top of the engine. In several weeks the locomotive will be ready for a cross country test run. I find the whole concept extremely exciting." Augustus replied, "Good job Jon, I will pass the information on to Mr. Neely. In the meantime, please document your findings."

The meeting with Jon gave Augustus the information he was looking for. The weak link in the engine was the piston compressors. If they became dysfunctional, the engine would fail. Now he had to find the guy who could successfully prevent operation of the compressors.

Giussepi Corleone immigrated to America from Sicily some 20 years ago. He borrowed from relatives and bought a pickup truck and started a trucking business hauling whatever he could. Through hard work and diligence he built a substantial trucking business that included several large 18 wheelers. Neely Chemicals had a long running contract with Giussepi for their trucking needs. In the old days, out of necessity, Giussepi did some hauling for the Mafia organization, but he slowly drifted away into everything legal. Augustus thought that Giussepi might help him find the right person to sabotage the Oil-Free locomotive. He realized the sensitivity of the request and that he had to approach the request indirectly and without mention of the objective. He must be very delicate in the conversation and hope that Giuseppe picks up on his hints.

During a standard trucking delivery to Neely Chemicals, Augustus approached Giussepi. "Giussepi, I have a favor to ask of you. I need your advice." Giuseppe responded, "Augustus, I provide trucking services, not advice."

Augustus, "I realize that, but I believe you are in a unique position to assist me."

Giussepi, "What is it Augustus, do you want me to move a relative?"

Augustus, "No, this is a serious matter. I was hoping you could provide contact information from long ago acquaintances. Perhaps, when you first came into this country."

Giussepi's face became very serious, with deeply furrowed brow. He suspected that Augustus was looking for some illegal adventure. He replied, "Augustus, for whatever you have in mind, I do not want to know. Here is the telephone number of someone who might help you, but you must keep my identity out of this. I have a clean substantial business and I want to keep it that way."

"Don't worry Giussepi, your name will never be mentioned and I thank you for your assistance."

Back in Lake Shore, PA, plans were being hatched for the cross country trial of the Oil-Free locomotive. The attendees included George Nation, CEO of Major Electric, Chris Conamacki, CEO of Cross Country Railroad and Wilson Shindler, CEO of Tribos Engineering. Mr. Conamacki had called the meeting. He presided with the following remarks, "We plan to drive the Oil-Free locomotive across country from Lake Shore to Portland, Oregon pulling a conventional diesel locomotive, which will act as a spare in case there is trouble with the Oil-Free engine. In Portland, a 20 car freight load will be hooked up and preparations made for the trip to Philadelphia. Two man crews are used to drive the train in 12 hour shifts. Each crew consists of an engineer and a fireman. The so called "fireman" is capable of driving the train, and the two men alternate in the driving position every 6 hours. For the last leg of the journey, from the Cleveland area to Philadelphia, we would like Wilson to join the crew as a big demonstration is planned when the train arrives in Philadelphia. We have made arrangements for the press and TV to be at the final destination, where a victory celebration is planned. Each of us is to speak for about 5 minutes. I will make the introductions. Please have your prepared remarks reviewed by our staff. Is this plan agreeable to you Wilson and you George?" Wilson replied, "Sounds great to me. I would love to have the opportunity to experience our engine in its actual operation. We do not get to do that very often." George also agreed and considered the publicity to be very beneficial to Major Electric. Chris concluded, "Great, Wilson please meet with Byron Jamison to obtain logistic information. We anticipate driving the engines to Portland next week and the train trip back will start on the following week. That gives us ample time to prepare for the reception, which will be taken care of by Cross Country Railroad. Publicity is paramount for this exercise. We want the world to know of our technical advancement and our contribution to energy preservation"

Wilson met with Byron Jamison of The Cross Country Railroad to discuss detailed logistics of the demonstration train. "Hi Wilson, I have been looking forward to meeting you. We are thrilled with the Oil-Free locomotive and we anticipate doing substantial business with Major Electric and Tribos Engineering. We would like you to meet the train just east of Cleveland. We anticipate that the train would reach Cleveland about October 18, two weeks from now. It will be quite late at night so that there should not be any spectators. You are to fly to Cleveland that evening. Someone will meet you at the airport and drive you to the pick-up destination. The forward entrance to the train leads to the engineer's area. There will be a folding chair and a sleeping bag for your use as desired. The run to Philadelphia will take approximately 12 hours. We will pay all expenses and make all travel arrangements to get to Philadelphia and to return home after the celebration. Do you have any questions? "Wilson replied, "Yes, I have one request. I would like to be accompanied by one of our technicians who has intimate knowledge of the engine, to witness performance in its actual setting. His name is Robert Carpone." Byron agreed, "Fine, I will double the arrangements."

On his trip back to New York, from Lake Shore, PA, Wilson composed his reception speech.

My name is Wilson Shindler, and I am President of Tribos Engineering, the inventors of the Oil-Free diesel. I had the opportunity and privilege to ride the last leg of the train's cross country journey from Portland Oregon. I am pleased to report that the engine performed flawlessly. The locomotive trip was more than a demonstration of the engine. It was the genesis of a revolutionary technology that will have a great transformation on our lives. Piston engines may not need the precious resource of oil, but can use the air around us as the lubricant. Not only did we demonstrate the engine itself, but also we demonstrated air lubricated piston compressors, that will also find numerous applications in the future. Our company is dedicated to advanced technology and we look forward to many more inventions that will benefit mankind. I want to thank Major Electric and Cross Country Railroad for their belief in our organization and for their unequivocal support. We also want to thank all of you who have come here today to participate in this wonderful celebration.

It was time now for Augustus to make his fateful telephone call. He dialed the number that Giussepi had given him. The response at the other end came after 5 rings, "yeah!" Augustus continued, "My name is Augustus Bolen and you have been recommended to perform a job I seek." The reply from the other end, "Who recommended me?" The accent was uncultured, and you might say typical gangland, and quite distinctive from Augustus.

Augustus, "I cannot divulge that information. I want to meet with you and explain what I have in mind. Considerable funds are involved." The response came slowly, as if after serious contemplation, "Meet me at Jake's Bar and Grill in Sucretville, on Tuesday at 7:30PM. I will be in a booth at the back. I will be wearing a black hoodie. Use my name as 'Smitty'." Then Augustus heard the hang-up click.

Augustus searched the telephone book for Jakes Bar and Grill. As he suspected, it was on the seedy part of town, but in an isolated neighborhood. He thought to himself, probably a good place to meet.

When Augustus went to work the following Monday, Horace asked, "How is your project faring?" Augustus replied "We are making progress and I will know more tomorrow."

After work on Tuesday, Augustus went home and changed to his jeans and flannel shirt. He had a weather worn leather jacket that he felt was proper for the occasion. Prior to going home that day he rented the cheapest car available for his trek to Sucretville.

Augustus arrived at the designated rendezvous at about 7:40 PM. He entered Jakes Bar and Grille. It was dimly lit and rather sparsely populated. At the bar was a macho man showing off his muscles to a scantily dressed woman who was obviously a prostitute. Augustus meandered to the back booths and saw a man enjoying a beer and dressed with a black hoodie. Augustus asked "Are you Smitty?" The man replied in a gruff tone, "That's what they call me. Sit down and tell me your story." Smitty was a big man with large shoulders and strong arms. He didn't have a beard, but he was not clean shaven. His eyes were beady and he had a wide nose that must have been broken several times. He looked the part of a typical thug, but his conversation, although terse was quite intelligent. Augustus continued, "I don't know if you are familiar with the Oil-Free locomotive that has been in the media lately. A demonstration of the locomotives freight carrying ability is scheduled to begin next week. It will be traveling from Portland, Maine, cross country to Philadelphia, PA. The group that I represent want the engine to fail before it reaches its destination. The engine requires high pressure air that is supplied by an Oil-Free piston compressor.

Sufficient damage to the compressor would cause engine failure. The failure must not appear as sabotage, but as a deficiency in the engine. Do you think that you can complete such a task?" Smitty considered the request for some time and responded, "I believe that I can complete that mission. I used to work on locomotives and have some familiarity with them. The job will cost $300,000, with $150,000 up front and the remainder after the mission is completed. Here is my bank and bank account. Transfer the upfront funds immediately. If the money does not appear, than the job will not be done." Augustus responded, "I understand. The money will be transferred tomorrow."

Augustus then left the premises and headed back to his condominium.

Smitty's real name was Pancho Contato. He was an illegal immigrant from Mexico where he was part of a drug cartel. Gangland in the states purchased him from the Conquisitor gang in Mexico. He was involved in several bank hoists and enemy gang murders, but he managed to survive law enforcements destruction of many of the gangs in the states. He then became a lone operator. He had no family, but was seen around town with several girlfriends. Pancho was a big man, with great strength and muscle. Besides his physical attributes he was very clever and intelligent. He was often called upon to execute various illicit jobs for which he was paid handsomely. As was done on all his jobs, he conducted intensive research. He read the magazine publications concerning the Oil-Free engine and whatever newspaper articles were presently available. He went to the public library and read and studied the micro-fiche articles and patents. After a week's time, Pancho was quite familiar with the engine and the compressors that supplied the high pressure air. What could he do to immobilize the compressor without being obvious sabotage? He decided to loosen the discharge piping flange attached to the compressor so that most of the compressed air would flow into the environment instead of the engine. He would need a large wrench and plenty of muscle.

Next, Pancho would have to set up his itinerary. He studied carefully what was in the public domain. In three days' time the locomotive would leave Portland, Oregon. In 7 days' time, a reception was to be held in Philadelphia about noon time. Following the railroad line maps that he had purchased, Pancho figured that the train would pass Cleveland about 1:00 AM. He wanted to enter the train in the black of night, so that he would be undetected, from the back door of the locomotive. Some 20 miles east of Cleveland, the train would pass a cross road. Pancho could park his car nearby and catch the train, which would be close to 2: AM. He

152

decided that he would drive to Cleveland and examine the terrain prior to the day of the event to ensure that his plan was correct. He even would watch the crossing in late evening to ensure that it was unpopulated as he suspected. Pancho also knew that the back door of the locomotive would be locked from the inside. Therefore, he would need an acetylene tank and burner hose and nozzle, so that he could burn out the lock and enable back door opening for his entrance. He believed he had everything figured out and he departed for his road trip to Cleveland.

Pancho arrived at the crossroad late in the evening and surveyed the terrain. A woods was nearby where he could hide his vehicle for subsequent pickup. A freight train passed by blew its whistle and slowed as it passed the cross road that had the automatic gates down. The slower pace of the train would enable Pancho to grab on without difficulty. Everything seemed in place for his sabotage venture.

Back home Wilson explained the railroad plan to Jim Clairborne and Bob Carpone. They loved the plan and more importantly to the publicity it would bring to the company. Jim decided to prepare for an onslaught of orders.

Soon, the time had come for Wilson and Bob Carpone to depart for Cleveland. They each had a small suitcase containing a change of clothing and toilet accessories. They were quite excited about the prospect of riding in a locomotive with the Oil-Free engine. The flight to Cleveland landed about 11:00 PM. Wilson and Bob were met by a representative from Cross Country Railroad. He drove the pair to the rendezvous area where they were to meet the train. They relaxed in a nearby all-night diner with pie and coffee until the train arrived. The Cross Country representative kept in contact by phone with the engineer and fireman who were driving the train, so that the precise meeting time could be designated.

Pancho also arrived at the railroad crossing and hid his vehicle in the woods. He chose a vantage point to observe the oncoming train that he would surreptitiously board. Pancho did see another car approach and park on the side pf the road. He wondered what they were doing.

About 1:00 AM, a train whistle was heard in the distance and if one looked down the tracks the engine headlights were visible. Pancho saw a group of men get out of the car that was parked on the side of the road. Two of the men were carrying suitcases. The train slowed down precipitously as it approached the crossing and then it came to a complete stop. The men with the suitcases shook hands with the driver of their car and they ascended the locomotive cab entrance at the front of the locomotive. How convenient, Pancho thought, I don't have to run for the train, I just have to sneak on the rear platform of the locomotive. Although the front of the locomotive was illuminated with a street light, the rear was not and it was easy for Pancho to climb the stairs to the rear platform. He was carrying with him a small acetylene tank and torch and a set of large ratchet wrenches. He knelt down as the train pulled away in a position that would make it hard to detect his presence. The other car made a U-Turn and pulled away. When darkness once again engulfed the locomotive, Pancho began to use the acetylene torch carefully to burn out the rear door lock. The rear door metal was quite thin and the burning operation went fast. Once Pancho could unlock the door he discarded the acetylene tank and hose and he entered the rear of the locomotive with his wrenches and closed the door behind him

Meanwhile, Wilson and Bob Carpone made their introductions to the engineer and fireman in the forward cab.

After some affable conversation, Wilson was anxious to observe the operation of the engine. He requested permission from the engineer who said "Sure, have a look. The engine has been running as smooth as silk." Wilson then entered the engine compartment. When Pancho saw Wilson, he immediately hid behind the machinery so that he was out of sight. Wilson began examining the various components of the engine. He observed the piston compressors at the top of the engine carefully. He saw that the main compressor was reciprocating smoothly, while the spare was idle. Wilson's concentration gave Pancho the opportunity to sneak behind Wilson and hit him hard with a black jack that he had in his pocket. Wilson immediately slumped to the floor unconscious and with a blood stain on his head. Pancho then ascended to the top of the engine to dismantle the operating compressor. There was insufficient clearance on top of the engine for Pancho to stand and he would have to loosen the discharge flange in a slightly kneeling position. He quickly surmised where the flange was and fitted a ratchet wrench into a bolt head. It took all his strength to loosen a bolt, but his adrelinine enabled him to make progress. Meanwhile, Bob Carbone was receiving information on how to run the locomotive from the engineer who was driving the train. He finally said, "I better go in the back and see what Wilson is doing." When Bob entered the engine compartment, he saw Wilson slumped on the ground. When he ran to attend to him a blackjack missile glazed the side of his head and Carpone was thrown to the floor. He then saw the culprit, namely Pancho on top of the engine. Lying on the floor next to Bob was a large Monkey Wrench. Bob picked up the wrench, stood up and with all his might threw the wrench at the intruder at the top of the engine. Bob Carpone had pitched in semi pro baseball and his throw at the intruder was a perfect shoulder follow through and an accurate strike. The wrench struck Pancho in the back of the head and he immediately was knocked cold and he laid prone on top of the engine. Pancho had done enough damage to the primary piston compressor to force the spare to activate and supply pressurized air to the engine. When this occurred, the primary compressor shut down. The compressors transition was flawless.

Although still in a daze, Carpone forced himself into the forward cab and related to the engineer that Wilson needed an ambulance and the police were needed to apprehend the intruder. The fireman then radioed to headquarters and a 911 call was forwarded to the closest emergency area. The instructions were for the train to halt at a crossing some 5 miles down the track. In the interim, Carpone attended to Wilson and himself with the available first aid kit aboard the train. Wilson had not recovered consciousness but Carpone could attend to his head wound and cauterize the bleeding. Pancho remained atop the engine, and still unconscious.

At the designated intersection, two ambulances and two police cars were waiting. Wilson was delivered to one ambulance and the intruder to the other, but under the custody of the police. In Wilson's ambulance his vitals were taken including blood pressure and lung examination. His vitals were normal, and Oxygen was administered. In the other ambulance, Pancho had regained consciousness and was handcuffed. He was also treated by emergency personnel. During the trip to Mercy Hospital, Wilson awakened and complained of a splitting headache. He was given Tylenol that eased the pain somewhat. At the hospital, Wilson was seen by a Neurologist who asked questions to see if his memory was affected. Wilson was well aware of what had happened, but the Neurologist recommended a Cat-Scan to determine if there was brain damage. The scan revealed a concussion, but no visible breakage damage to the skull. He was to remain in the hospital for observation and treatment.

Meanwhile, the train proceeded on its way to Philadelphia. Bob Carpone had remained on the train and applied an antiseptic and band aid to the slight scrape on his forehead. The train was scheduled to arrive in Philadelphia at

8:30 AM. A large contingent of dignitaries and spectators was scheduled to meet the "Oil-Free train". It was important that it not be late. The engineer increased the speed of the locomotive above normal so as to meet the announced arrival. The engine did not hesitate and easily met the increased speed. Chris Conamacki of Cross Country Railroad and George Nation of Major Electric had been advised of the attempted sabotage and they requested that Bob Carpone prepare remarks to substitute for Wilson. Bob spent some time reviewing Wilson's speech and began the necessary embellishment including the reasons for Wilson's absence. He had some 6 or 7 hours to prepare, which certainly was sufficient time, but Bob was not accustomed to public speaking. After all, he was a technician with a two year degree from a community college. Never the less, Bob had an outgoing personality and although he had some trepidation, he looked forward to the opportunity.

At precisely 8:30 AM the train pulled into the Philadelphia station. A 12 man band began playing patriotic music and the TV cameras and commentators began reporting. A huge throng of spectators cheered wildly and waved American flags. It was a scene almost reminiscent of the celebration after the end of World War 2. Chris Conamacki began the speeches, extolling the virtues and benefits to the railroad of the Oil-Free engine. George Nation spoke on behalf of Major Electric, stating that he expected all future locomotives from his company to be Oil-Free and how he considered the technical achievement to be monumental. Then it was time for Bob to give his speech. He proceeded as follows:

My name is Bob Carpone and I am an employee of the Tribos Engineering Company, the inventor of the Oil-Free engine. The real brains behind the engine is our president Wilson Shindler. The invention has aroused world-wide attention and has placed substantial demands on Mr. Shindler's activities and that is why he could not be with you today. He asked me to pass on the following remarks:

"The locomotive trip was more than a demonstration of the engine. It was the genesis of a revolutionary technology that will have a great transformation on our lives. Piston engines may not need the precious resource of oil, but can use the air around us as the lubricant. Not only did we demonstrate the engine itself, but also we demonstrated an Oil-Free air lubricated piston compressor, that will also find numerous applications in the future. Our company is dedicated to advanced

technology and we look forward to many more inventions that will benefit mankind. I want to thank Major Electric and Cross Country Railroad for their belief in our organization and for their unequivocal support. We also want to thank all of you who have come here today to participate in this wonderful celebration"

The reception continued for another two hours. Finger food and punch was provided and the company executives and Bob Carpone mingled easily with the crowd. It was quite amazing that Bob, a hands –on technician, had the social acumen to give an excellent speech and handle himself with great social dexterity at the reception. He was confronted with numerous questions about the engine, and since he had intimate knowledge, answered all without hesitation. He became a great representative for Tribos engineering. While still at the reception, Bob received a cell phone message from Jim Clairborne. "Bob, please return to Mercy hospital to be with Wilson Shindler. When he is released, I want you to accompany him home. I believe auto would be the best mode of transportation, as airport crowds and hype would be too much for him at the present time. I have spoken to the doctors at the hospital. Wilson has a concussion and needs rest and peace and quiet. Please rent a comfortable auto and drive back to the hospital. Also, Wilson's wife Maureen wants to be with Wilson. Travel arrangements are being made for her to fly to Cleveland. Pick her up at the airport and make whatever hotel reservations are required. Talk to the doctor's at the hospital and get the low down on Wilson, etc. It is vitally important to our company that Wilson return to good health. I am depending on you Bob, and I have complete confidence in your abilities. Please keep me informed."

Pancho was brought to police headquarters in East Cleveland. There he was met by FBI personnel John Morrison and William Acker. Pancho refused to talk and remained silent to this point. He carried no identification so the local police didn't know who he was. He was brought into a conference room for further questioning by the FBI agents. Since the crime was committed in a vehicle that crossed state lines, he could be accused of a federal offense, and the FBI had jurisdiction. Morrison began the interrogation with the Miranda rights. "You have the right to remain silent and anything you say could be used against you in court. You have the right to consult with an attorney and to have that attorney present during questioning. Your name is Pancho Contato, and you live in the capital district of New York State." Pancho responded, "How do you know my name?" Morrison replied, "You left your car at the site where you boarded the train and we traced your license plate to your personal information. You are in serious trouble Pancho, being accused of attempted murder, destruction of private property and endangerment. For your information, you could be behind bars for 20 years. The only way your sentence could be reduced is by a plea bargain. We know that your savings account was increased by some $150,000 several days before your escapade. Someone paid you off to commit the crime. Give us the details and your punishment could be reduced." Pancho replied, "I am not talking. I want a lawyer to defend me."

DIAGNOSIS

Bob Carpone rented a luxury car for the trip back to Mercy hospital. It was a good 10 hour drive and the comfort of the luxury vehicle was most welcome. Bob was very tired. He had little sleep for the last several days. The music from the Bose speakers was very soothing, but Bob made sure to stop at every roadside restaurant along the way to get a cup of coffee to ensure that he would not fall asleep at the wheel. The car also included safeguards such as lane detectors and laser controls against frontal crashes. The installed GPS kept him from getting lost as he traversed a path to the selected hotel near the hospital. Along the way, Bob thought about Wilson. He considered Wilson a genius and absolutely essential to the well-being of the company. Tears welled in his eyes as he thought about Wilson's concussion and what it might do to his creativity. As he drove his thoughts concentrated around Wilson, how he built a company from scratch, how he developed porous bearing technology, how he developed a gas bearing rotary table, how he developed a successful exclusion seal, and of course his major contribution being an Oil-Free piston engine. Through it all Wilson treated his employees very well. Carpone's thoughts made the time pass quickly and soon he was at the entrance to the designated hotel. He checked in at the lobby counter, went to his room, put a "Do Not Disturb" sign on the door, undressed and plopped down on the bed. He was fast asleep in five minutes.

The next morning Carpone awoke at about 9:00AM. He showered, shaved and dressed casually. He was to pick up Maureen at the Cleveland Airport at about 3:00 PM. The airport was a good hour's drive from the hotel. After a hearty breakfast at the hotel, Carpone wandered over to Mercy Hospital to visit with Wilson. Carpone was advised that Wilson was in the Intensive Care Unit and was only allowed a fifteen minute visit. Wilson was lying in bed, but awake, with intravenous tubes and electronic monitoring equipment attached to his body. When Wilson eyed Bob he sat up in his bed, "Hi Bob, it is good to see you. I heard you did a wonderful job at the reception." Carpone replied, "I just read what you had written. I will be leaving in a little while to pick up your wife at the Cleveland airport. How are you feeling?" Wilson answered, "I am ok, but extremely tired. That guy, whoever he was gave me a good whack. I am quite anxious to get back to work as I know there is lots of activity. I am also anxious to see my wife Maureen again. She has been such a good partner." Bob conjectured, "Wilson, the doctors stated that you need complete rest for quite a while. Jim Clairborne has things under control at the plant. When you are ready to leave here, we will motor in a luxury car back to New York, so as to avoid the commotions at the airports." Wilson heard the commentary and in his mind agreed with it, but tiredness took over and he slumped to sleep." Bob left the room and prepared for his trip to the Cleveland Airport.

Wilson was supposed to give his mind a rest, but his mind did not cooperate. Although Wilson was in a deep sleep his mind was active. His thoughts retraced the development of his company, Tribos Engineering. He remembered his presentation at Mechanical Analytics for the development of an Oil-Free engine and the subsequent rejection. He chuckled in his sleep and thought they should see me now. The development of the gas bearing rotary tables came to mind and the patent dispute that ensued. Then, the Venture Capitalists that tried to take over our company and sell our resources for a quick buck. He could only imagine what the attack and destruction on the train was all about, but he believed that it had something to do with the removal of oil from the diesel engine. It seemed to Wilson that ethics and common sense was not too prevalent in the corporate world. But then he thought of Major Electric and Cross Country Railroad who were very ethical and even generous with their relations with Tribos Engineering.

His thoughts than drifted to his wife Maureen. It has been almost ten years since Wilson went into his own business.

During that time he worked incessantly, during the day at the office, and at night at home. It suddenly occurred to Wilson that he had been neglecting his wife. They hadn't vacationed over that period. Going out to dinner was a rare occurrence and similarly going to a movie. Maureen understood his situation and loyally supported his activities, because she loved him dearly and wanted him to succeed. But in his sleep, he vowed to be a more attentive husband and father to his son Gregory who was a doctor in Boston. Wilson then fell into a deep blank sleep without mind thoughts or dreams.

Carpone parked the luxury vehicle in the Cleveland Airport short term lot about ½ hour before Maureen's plane was scheduled to land and went to the gate to greet her when she disembarked. Bob was advised by Jim Clairborne that Maureen was informed with the situation and the attack on Wilson. Maureen recognized Bob Carpone and they greeted each other warmly. "What is the situation with Wilson?" Maureen asked. Carpone replied, "He has a concussion and is in observation at the intensive care unit at the hospital. The Doctor's indicate that he needs peace and quiet for a period of time until his head feels better and he returns to normal. He is expected to remain hospitalized for several more days and then the three of us will drive back to New York." Maureen contemplated, "Why would anyone attack Wilson, his creativity is good for mankind. I do not know how anyone can hold him down, his mind is so active."

Maureen and Carpone arrived at Mercy Hospital about 4:30 PM. They went directly to the ICU to visit with Wilson. Wilson's eyes lit up when he saw Maureen and he extended his arms to greet her. She hugged and kissed him and he commented on how good she looked. She replied "makeup can cover everything." Wilson countered, "Maybe I should get some makeup. How are things on the home front?" Maureen responded, "Everything is under control. All the bills are being paid. I miss making supper for you. I understand that you will be here for several more days and then we will drive home with Bob Carpone." Wilson had a wry smile on his face. "Do you mean you and me alone in the back of the car? I am afraid that I won't be able to do anything." Maureen replied, "Wilson, we haven't done anything in years. Don't worry about it." Bob Carpone had a big smile as he enjoyed the kidding conversation. Some 10 minutes later, the visitors were asked to leave, as the regimen for Wilson was complete rest.

Maureen and Carpone were in the waiting room when Dr. Jurgens, the neurologist appeared to give them the status of Wilson. "Mr. Shindler has a serious concussion, but there was no breakage of the skull or brain. He has a good chance of complete recovery, but in order for the brain to heal it cannot be over worked. My recommendations is complete rest for the next two months. He should not go to his office or be involved in any way with his company. We anticipate him leaving the hospital in three days." Maureen interjected, "Dr., Wilson's mind is never still. It will be impossible for him to be blank. What happens if he continues to be involved with his company?" The doctor replied, "It is hard to predict. It is possible that he could have a relapse that could produce permanent damage. On the other hand, it is possible he could return to a normal state. It depends on the strength of his mind. The safest course of action is complete quiet to let the brain recover slowly and surely. I suggest that you visit a neurologist in New York. We can provide doctor recommendations and we can supply all the medical records that were made here. I have advised the nurses here to allow extended visits of ½ hour duration for as long as he will be here. I wish you the best of luck."

Afterwards when Bob and Maureen separated, Bob put in a call to Jim Clairborne at the headquarters of Tribos Engineering. "Jim, the doctor is pretty insistent that Wilson rest without taxing his mind. Maureen thinks that might be very difficult."

Clairborne responded, "That is very unfortunate because there are some very key decisions facing us and Wilson is the only one who can decide. We will have to play it by ear and do the best that we can. When do you expect him to leave the hospital?"

Carpone responded," My best guess would be in two days and we would start our drive home on the third day. He may be available to talk to on the fourth day."

Clairborne closed, "Thanks Bob, I will see you at the end of the week."

PLEA BARGAIN

Julius Destafano entered the police station in Clarksville where Pancho was being held. Julius was heavy set bordering on obesity. His face had large eyes and deep jowls around the mouth. He had small diamond ear rings in the lobes of each ear. He wore a grey vested suit with decorative handkerchiefs emanating from the lapel pocket. "Good morning, my name is Julius Destafano and I am Pancho Contato's attorney." The police man receptionist responded, "Please wait here while I get the chief." Julius and the chief entered the chief's office and held a discussion for more than half an hour. Afterwards, Julius was escorted to Pancho's cell. "Hello Pancho, you seem to have gotten yourself in some serious trouble." Pancho responded, "Can the mob help me out?" Destafano replied, "I am afraid not. You know the rules Pancho. If you solo you are on your own, and you soloed. Now here is the situation. You were found on top of the engine and photographs were taken. Your finger prints are on the wrench you were using and on the flange you were loosening. Your blackjack has hairs from Mr. Shindler's head. Your car was found hidden in the woods where you boarded the train. The purchase of an acetylene tank was traced to your credit card. Your actions were witnessed by Mr. Shindler and his assistant. You really do not have a prayer. My advice is to engage in a plea bargain to have your sentence reduced. I personally can no longer be involved. I will report your situation to Don Giovani. Good luck." Julius then left the cell and the police station and headed back to his office in New York.

THE RIDE HOME

The time had come for Wilson to leave the hospital. His health situation had greatly improved to the surprise of the doctors. Wilson was anxious to get back to New York and to his company. He knew that there would be extensive activity after the successful demonstration of the Oil-Free engine and many decisions would have to be made. He wanted to discuss the situation with Jim Clairborne as quickly as possible. Maureen and Bob Carpone did their best to hold him down.

It was a 10 hour drive back to New York provided food and bathroom stops were not too long. Wilson still showed signs of tiredness, but he was very fidgety as the trip progressed. "Bob, can you get Jim Clairborne on the phone. I have to know what is happening with Tribos Engineering. I am sure that after the demonstration, there must be lots of activity." Bob responded, "I can't get him on the phone right now. I have to concentrate on driving as there is lots of traffic on this highway." Maureen interjected, "Wilson, you will have plenty of time to catch up when we get home. As per the doctor's orders, you are to put your mind at rest." It didn't matter what Maureen said as Wilson fell asleep again with his head supported by the hospital pillow.

During stops at the highway restaurants, Wilson was able to walk straight, use the rest room and eat a sandwich.

Maureen was somewhat amazed at his recovery. Again he asked to speak to Jim Clairborne. Carpone replied, "I left the phone in the car. We can call when we get back there." When they returned to the car, Wilson slumped in the back seat and went to sleep. Maureen commented. "Bob you are doing a great job of fending off Wilson. I hope you can keep it up."

An hour later, Wilson awakened and this time he was insistent. "Bob, give me your phone and don't put me off." Carpone realized that he had no choice and he gave his cell phone to Wilson. Maureen admonished, "Wilson, if you don't obey the doctor's orders, your mind can get worse and you will be laid off longer." Wilson retorted, "My mind is fine. I just need to make one call." Wilson checked his watch and surmised that Jim Clairborne was still in the office. He dialed his number. "Hello Jim, Wilson here. I'm OK but the doctor recommends complete rest, which is very hard for me to do. I plan on staying home for the rest of this week. Come visit me and brief me on what is going on. I have one immediate request. I don't want the sabotage to make the media news as it takes away from the successful demonstration of the Oil-Free engine. Please coordinate with Major Electric and Cross Country Railroad and express my wishes on this matter. If the press asks about me, tell them I am recuperating from a bad cold. I expect to be home in 4 or 5 hours and we can talk again tomorrow." Clairborne replied, "Don't worry Wilson. George Nation of Major Electric and Chris Conamacki of Cross Country Railroad had the same thoughts and wanted to keep sabotage quiet. We will do our best to keep the press out of it. In the meantime the Oil-Free demonstration with the cross country run has been a great success. I will brief you on what is going on when we get together. In the meantime get some rest and come back here refreshed. We need you like never before. So long for now."

Maureen was amazed at Wilson's facility to immediately grasp the situation and come to a decision. She thought to herself, "There is no way that Wilson Shindler's mind can be inactive and he will overpower any mind damage. Welcome home Wilson!" Wilson returned the phone to Carpone and chatted with Maureen. "You know Maureen, business has been a great detriment to our relationship. I promise I will find more time for us to do things together like we used to. In the hospital, I dreamt that I had been neglecting you and it bothered me. You have been so loyal to me. Please forgive me and I promise to be more attentive to you and our son." Maureen became teary eyed and replied, "Dear Wilson. I know what you have been going through, and I greatly admired your abilities. I was thinking, I married an Icon, and I will suffer the consequences whatever that may be. I want you to know that I am very proud of you and I will be at your side no matter what." Wilson then held her in his arms for the remainder of the trip.

A SURPRISE VISITOR

Augustus Bolen knew the sabotage plan had failed, but he did not know the details. He had no communication with Pancho. Horace Neeley was extremely nervous and kept bugging Augustus, "Have you heard anything from your guy who was supposed to stop the Oil-Free engine during the cross country trip?" Augustus replied, "Haven't heard a thing yet. All we know is his venture failed and we are out $150,000. I will let you know as soon as I can find out anything."

Perry Donaldson had been with the FBI for some 25 years. He operated out of the upper New York State Office. His mission today was to pick up Augustus Bolen and bring him in for questioning at the nearest FBI facility. Since the FBI always worked in pairs or more, his partner in this mission was Jonathan Culver.

The two FBI agents arrived at Neeley Chemicals about 10:30 AM. They flashed their badges to the receptionist and asked to see Augustus Bolen. The receptionist became rather flustered and replied, "Gentlemen, please wait here." She then scurried out to advise her supervisor of the visitors. The supervisor, Mary Mckinley, then approached the agents, "Gentlemen, may I be of service?" Donaldson again flashed his badge and replied, "Madam, we are from the FBI, and we want to talk to Augustus Bolen. Now stop putting us off or you can be held in contempt."

After considerable scurrying behind the scenes, Augustus finally emerged. "I understand that you gentlemen wanted to see me." Donaldson inquired, "Are you Augustus Bolen?" Augustus answered, "That's me." Donaldson interjected, "I have a warrant for your arrest. You are accused of being an accomplice to attempted murder, destruction of private property and reckless endangerment. You have a right to remain silent, but anything you say can be held against you. You also have a right to legal representation. Now, please accompany us to the nearest FBI facility."

Augustus replied. "This is ridiculous. You have the wrong man. I have done nothing wrong and have been diligently working at my job every day. I am sure that we can straighten this mistake out very quickly." He was then escorted out of the premises and placed in the FBI car.

Horace Neeley had witnessed the entire incident from his overlooking balcony. He was in a cold sweat and then retired to the executive men's room where he threw up.

THE BUSINESS PLAN

Wilson rested at home for several days, and made considerable progress in his health and the way that he felt. He generally read the paper in the morning and did the jumble and crossword. He watched several sports programs on TV and he felt that he had done enough resting. He was anxious to get back to the office and continue to lead his company. Maureen recommended additional time off but she did recognize his anxiety and reflected that maybe he would be better off going back to work. The call was made by Wilson to Jim Clairborne. "Jim, this is Wilson here. I would like you to drop by tomorrow to discuss the status of our business. Let's make it around 10: AM, and we will have prepared sandwiches with trimmings for lunch. Maureen will be teaching at school." Clairborne replied, "Great, Wilson, we have lots to talk about. Looking forward to seeing you tomorrow."

The next day Clairborne arrived at the Shindler residence precisely at 10:00 AM. After pleasantries were exchanged, they went into the kitchen and each had coffee. Jim began, "Since the successful cross country train ride, activity has been over whelming. The Major Electric contract has been extended to include all future locomotive diesels, and Cross Country Railroad wants all their diesels retrofitted. We are hiring new people and purchasing equipment so that we can meet the demand. We really need your leadership and creativity for the high volume production anticipated ahead. There are two other matters of significance. George Nation CEO of Major Electric says they want to invest in our company, and as soon as you feel up to it they would like a presentation of our Business Plan. The second item is that the Wall Investment Bank thinks that we should consider going public with an Initial Product Offering (IPO) and they want to be the underwriters. They claim that we could end up with a significant amount of cash, which is sorely needed now." Wilson smiled, "Business Plan! We really have none. Everything we have done has been AD-HOC. I guess it might not be a bad idea to have some kind of documented plan. Generating a plan might not be a bad thing to do while I am recuperating. So let's split our activities. I probably have to stay home for several weeks, during which time I can generate a business plan. Jim, you take over the responsibility for the IPO and negotiate with the bank. Keep me advised. I would want to know how much money we could raise and what the plus and minuses are. After all that I have been through, I would hate to lose control of the company to greedy stockholders. I would need to have a majority stake." Clairborne replied, "Sounds good to me. One other thing

Wilson. So far the sabotage attempt has been kept quiet. However, I have learned that perpetrators are being found, and a grand jury is likely. When that happens, I believe the press would get into the act and the story could go public." Wilson thought and then retorted, "You know we had a successful demonstration in spite of the effort to destroy the engine. That's because we had a backup compressor. I don't think that kind of press would hurt us, but might be helpful." Clairborne concluded, "Looks like we both have our work cut out for us. It is good to see you Wilson. I believe that your mind is as sharp as ever and I look forward to the day that you return to the plant."

After Clairborne left, Wilson began thinking about the business plan. The more he thought about it, the more he enjoyed the possibility. He said to himself, "I know what we have to do. Maybe it is a good idea to document our thinking and then communicate not only to Major Electric but to our own employees as well." He then went upstairs to his computer and started a Power Point presentation.

INITIAL PUBLIC OFFERING (IPO)

Jim Clairborne was asked to attend a meeting with Julius Bergdoff of the Wall Bank. The subject was an Initial Public Offering (IPO). The Wall Bank is a multinational institution with offices all over the world. Jim traveled to New York City and met Mr. Bergdoff at the Wall Bank Building. "Mr. Clairborne, it is kind of you to travel here and meet with me. Your company has recently enjoyed considerable positive publicity concerning the Oil-Free engine. Your management should be thinking of ways to capitalize on that publicity. One possibility is to add additional capital by offering stock to the public." Clairborne responded, "Presently our company is privately held, but we are always looking for ways to increase our capital backlog so that we can increase production and sales. We are novices when it comes to an Initial Public Offering (IPO) and I am here to learn what is involved."

Bergdoff remarked, "It is good that you study the procedure before you decide to do it. The procedure is quite involved and takes considerable effort on the company's part. Some of the big companies hire outside consulting organizations to assemble all the information required. I would also advise you that the process is not cheap and would probably cost some 10 percent of the dollar amount of the IPO. We have assembled descriptive material to guide you in the process. Please study it carefully and comply with the requirements. When you are ready for an underwriter then get back to me. In the interim do not hesitate to call me with any questions you may have."

A notebook with descriptive material was given to Jim. He thanked Bergdoff for his time and indicated that he would get back to him after studying the document.

On the flight back home, Jim began to peruse the notebook.

Management Senior management must have considerable financial and accounting experience to comply with the complex requirements that have been imposed by the SEC and by the Sarbanes-Oxley law. The composition of the board of directors must contain a majority of independent directors.

Financial Controls Stringent financial controls are required that must be approved by the SEC. An outside accounting firm is usually hired to set up the financial system. Also an outside auditor and legal firm is required to approve the procedures prior to submittal to the SEC.

Financial Reporting The manner in which the financial results are reported must also meet stringent requirements and are subject to similar scrutiny as described in Financial Controls.

Registration Statement The form S-1 registration statement is required by the SEC. The statement must contain the company's business model and overview of the future. How will the company use the proceeds from the sale of stock? Information regarding company officers and Board of Directors, including executive compensation must be supplied. A whole host of financial information for the past five years is required. The statement must be approved by the SEC and the information audited by an SEC approved agency.

Selection of Underwriter The underwriter does the actual selling of the stock. For Tribos that would be the Wall Bank who have already made contact.

Prospectus and printing Public information is generated through a prospectus. The prospectus contains a description of the company's business, financial statements, biographies of officers and directors, detailed information about their compensation, and a listing of material properties including patents. After the prospectus is completed it must be sent out to an approved printing company.

IPO Price The stock price is determined by the value of the company and the number of shares involved. In general a price between $14 and $16 dollars is optimum and the Net Present Value of the company is determined by studies conducted by investment bankers. The number of shares to be offered are adjusted to meet an optimum offering price.

IPO Road Show The stock will be sold to investment bankers who will in turn sell to their selected customer base and then to the public. The process involves presentations and travel to the various investment banks who might be interested.

Back home Jim continued studying the process involved in issuing an IPO. He concluded that the process is complex, long, time wise, and quite expensive. Clairborne was sure Wilson would not like the process and may not be amenable to going public.

The following day Jim Clairborne met with Wilson, who was still at home recovering from his concussion. Jim Clairborne carefully and thoroughly went through the various steps in the IPO process. Wilson seemed overwhelmed and he remarked, "Wow that is a difficult process and would consume much of yours and my time. What would we get out of all of this?" Clairborne answered, "We would shoot for 60 million. However that would not be net because there are considerable expenses involved. There is the underwriter discount, legal, accountant, printing fees and roadshow expenses plus quite a few others. Total IPO fees could exceed 10% of the gross proceeds." Wilson concluded, "Let's hold the IPO in abeyance. We have to see what Major Electric has in mind. By the way, the date for the Business Plan presentation has been set for two weeks from today at their headquarters in New Jersey. I would like you to attend with me. Also, put in writing what you have learned about an IPO so that I can study it some more. I plan to get back at work next week." Clairborne responded, "That sounds great Wilson. You have been dearly missed at Tribos. The place has not been the same without you."

SABOTAGE PUBLICITY

Once again the normal business din of Neeley Chemicals was disturbed by federal T men or by a more familiar name the FBI. The same personnel that came for Augustus, namely agents Perry Donaldson and Jonathan Culver entered the executive offices of Neeley Chemicals. Once again the receptionist scurried to get her supervisor, Mary McKinley. "Hello Gentlemen, you are back again. What is it this time?" Donaldson replied, "We are here to take Horace Neeley to headquarters." Mary responded, "There must be some mistake. Mr. Neeley is our Chief Executive Officer." Donaldson interjected, "Nevertheless Mary he is wanted for questioning in connection with an attempted sabotage of the Oil-Free train. It would behoove you to quietly fetch him and not disturb the staff." Several minutes later Horace appeared looking ashen and in a cold sweat." "Gentlemen, what can I do for you?" Donaldson replied, "Mr. Neeley you are being accused of being an accomplice to attempted murder, destruction of private property and reckless endangerment. You have a right to remain silent, but anything you say can be held against you and you have a right to legal counsel when being questioned." By this time, Horace was in a deep panic and he spurted out, "I had nothing to do with the attempted sabotage of the Oil-Free train. Augustus acted on his own, unbeknown to me." Donaldson continued, "Nevertheless, my orders are to take you in for questioning. I suggest you come along peacefully and not make a scene. You may make your explanations at headquarters." The three men left in the FBI car with Horace and Jonathan in the back seat and Perry driving.

Stanislaus Neeley, the founder of the company and principal stockholder and Horace's father took over leadership of the company during Horace's absence. When he learned of the charges against Horace and Augustus, he was livid with rage. He had no intention of using his influence to aid Horace and believed that Horace, if guilty, should take his punishment. In any event, Horace was to be replaced immediately. His message to the employees was as follows:

Fellow Employees – As you know Horace Neeley is presently under suspicion of abetting sabotage of the Oil-Free Train, ostensibly because Oil-Free would destroy our diesel oil additive business. If these allegations are true, then our company is in a very compromising position. We have never been involved in illegal activities and we have always prided ourselves on our ethical behavior. We are presently considering other candidates to take over leadership of the company. I have always believed in promoting from within and there are several promising candidates from within our company who are knowledgeable about our product mix and production procedures. Further advisements will follow.

The press, naturally jumped all over the story. Headlines in the local newspaper read:

Neely Chemical involved in sabotage of the Oil-Free train.

The paper went on to describe the three principals involved, namely, Horace, Augustus, and Pancho and that plea bargains were used to implicate the Neeley personnel. Reporters who dug into the case were able to determine details from a whistle blower on the grand jury. They found out what happened on the train and that Wilson Shindler suffered a concussion from a blow delivered by Pancho. They also were advised that the backup compressor system was activated and saved the engine from failure.

The press releases brought additional fame to Tribos Engineering and to Wilson personally. He was requested to appear on numerous TV and radio talk shows and he refused them all. He only commented to the press that he had recovered from his concussion and was returning to Tribos as CEO. The publicity was not only local but national and it favorably impacted additional business activity for Tribos Engineering.

Stanislaus realized that his company was viewed in an unfavorable light and he wanted to stem the tide, but before doing that he had one phone call to make. His secretary dialed the number and he was on the phone to Wilson Shindler. "Mr. Shindler, I am Stanislaus Neeley, the owner of Neeley Chemicals. I am thoroughly ashamed and disgusted at the behavior of my son Horace and Augustus Bolen in their attempt to sabotage the Oil-Free train. My company understands innovation since we do it all the time and we should never discourage it. What can I do to make up for the disaster caused by my company? I am willing to go as high as a million dollars in compensation." Wilson replied, "I was not planning on any legal action and I appreciate your offer. I am not sure that you are aware that we do business with your company. Neeley Chemicals provides us with the C-5 resin that we use with our porous carbon applications. The resin required development on your part to meet our requirements." Stanislaus was surprised to hear that Tribos Engineering was a customer and he could not believe Horace's stupidity to do harm to a customer. He replied, "That is interesting, Mr. Shindler. Rest assured, you will be getting a good deal for future orders of the resin. (In his mind, Stanislaus decided that he would supply the resin free of charge.). I want to commend you on your Oil-Free innovation. That will have tremendous ramifications on the transportation industry." Wilson continued, "Stanislaus, our company is in a transition period. We are considering going public with an IPO. I know your company is privately held and your experience could provide valuable insight to us. I believe that I would enjoy meeting you and discussing our options." Stanislaus replied, "I would very much enjoy meeting with you and I could provide you with our company history and background. I can tell you, it was not always smooth sailing. Let's set up a date when we can meet." Wilson replied, "Right now we are in the midst of collecting data and examining our options. I will contact you before we make a decision, and I very much appreciate your call." Stanislaus replied, "I look forward to meeting with you. Goodbye for now."

It was time for Stanislaus to air his feelings to the public. He called for a press conference at the Neeley Chemical facility. It was to be held in the large conference room, with a theatre seating arrangement. National television was invited.

An overflow crowd attended, including local and national newspapers and television. Appropriate microphones and speakers had been set up. The appointed time was 10:00 AM and Stanislaus appeared precisely on time and went directly to the podium.

I have a statement to make and afterwards I will honor a few questions.

As you know allegations have been filed against several employees of Neeley Chemicals, for attempted sabotage of the Oil-Free train during the trains cross country demonstration trip. One of the alleged perpetrators is my son Horace. I am appalled and ashamed that our company would be engaged in such an activity. We pride ourselves on innovation and we should rejoice if others can produce significant accomplishments in that regard. During the train trip an altercation occurred between members of the staff of Tribos Engineering and the criminal who was attempting the espionage. Mr. Wilson Shindler, the CEO of Tribos Engineering suffered a concussion during the melee. His associate brought the criminal down and he was placed in police custody. Operation of the engine was not affected because back- up systems were energized. I have spoken to Wilson Shindler and we agreed to continue future discussions on a variety of topics including appropriate compensation for the damage that was caused.

I have appointed Dr. Jeffery Newell as President of Neeley Chemicals. Dr. Newell has been an employee for over 20 years and has been responsible for many of the inventions and patents produced by the company. I have full confidence in his ability to run and grow our company. Now, I can entertain a few questions.

A reporter from the Associated Press asked. "Mr. Neeley, Will you be involved in the legal proceedings against your son Horace?" Stanislaus replied, "I do not know how I could be involved. Horace has his own lawyer. Presently, a Grand Jury is determining his involvement and whether he will be charged with a crime. Whatever the outcome, he will not return to the employ of Neeley Chemicals." The press conference lasted another 20 minutes, without any new information, from what was stated in the initial statement.

PLAN PRESENTATION

The drive to New Jersey was rather pleasant. It was the fall season and the trees were changing color. Although the temperature was brisk, the sun was shining and the drive proceeded along the more scenic areas in New Jersey. Jim Clairborne was driving and Wilson was in the front passenger seat. They were headed to Major Electric's executive offices to present the Business Plan that Wilson had conjured up while recuperating at home.

After several hours, they entered the gates of Major Electric headquarters, where they were confronted by a security guard. After providing their names to the security guard they were directed to the visitors parking location. The building was not palatial, but it did present an elitist structure with emphasis on the Grecian columns at the main entrance. The receptionist told the twosome to be seated in the lobby and an escort would arrive shortly and take them to the meeting room. When they arrived at the meeting room, George Nation, the CEO of Major Electric, provided a warm welcome and offered coffee and donuts, which were declined. Introductions were made all around. The managers of every division of Major Electric were in attendance, including their energy turbo generator business, their airplane engine business and of course, their locomotive business.

George Nation started the proceedings with some introductory remarks. "As we all know, Tribos Engineering developed an Oil-Free diesel engine, which we are using on our locomotives. During a demonstration train trip, Wilson Shindler, President of Tribos suffered a concussion from an attempted sabotage of the engine. We hope he has fully recovered. He has graciously accepted our invitation to present the Tribos Business Plan, because we may have interest in investing in Tribos. It is now eleven AM and I fully expect his discussion and the questions afterwards would run into our lunch period. Therefore we will break for an hour at noon and reconvene at 1:00 PM. Wilson, the floor is yours."

Wilson proceeded to bring up his presentation on the set-up laptop and turn on the connected projector.

"Thank you George. Let me start out by saying we have had excellent relations with Major Electric during our development of the Oil-Free engine and we look forward to a continuing relationship whether it be just with the engine or otherwise. I have developed a slide presentation and as we move along slides will appear concerning the subject matter I am talking about.

Let me begin with some history. How did Tribos Engineering evolve into what it is today? The first slide shows the company I worked for some ten years ago. Mechanical

Analytics was a research and development firm. The core of the company consisted of some high powered engineers and scientists, most with advanced degrees. We existed via contract work with industry and government. For some ten years, I enjoyed working with that company and I seriously thought that I would retire as a Mechanical Analytics employee. Unfortunately, the company ran into financial difficulty and declared bankruptcy. I felt somewhat betrayed, and I resigned to become a private consultant. As an aside, I did propose to management of Mechanical Analytics that we consider the development of an Oil-Free engine, but financial constraints prohibited research.

As a consultant, my first two jobs was to complete some work that I was involved in at Mechanical Analytics. One of these jobs was completion of a report for preliminary work on a helium buffer seal for NASA. The other job, as shown on the screen was for a gas bearing machine tool spindle. For my private consulting practice, I had sent out literature describing my capabilities and background to prospective clients. As a result of my private marketing I received a call from Jason Terwilliger the CEO of Advanced Machine Tool Company. (Name and company shown on screen) He was interested in my background in Gas Bearings and in particular he wanted to know if I had any ideas about

196

supporting large rotary tables on gas bearings. A big advantage of gas bearings for large rotary tables was position accuracy. His company tried the same schemes used by small tables with abject failure. We came up with the scheme shown on the next slide. It consisted of a series of separate pads, which were hydrostatically energized by supply air pressure. For high stiffness and load capacity the pads were arranged at the periphery of the table rather than on the drive shaft. The pad interface consisted of porous carbon impregnated with a resin. The resin was carefully applied to provide the proper pressure drop between the supply and the film. Half the pads were free floating and half were fixed. That arrangement permitted the pads to operate at the small films required for adequate stiffness and allow for the accommodation of centrifugal and thermal expansion of the table. Mr. Terwilliger thought the idea was worth pursing and contracted me to build and test the system. I had several people helping me, on a contract basis, to design and build the system. Whatever money I needed was supplied by Advanced Machine Tool Company (AMT). Mr. Terwilliger did not believe in hiring his own people to produce the bearing system. The next slide shows the initial bearing system installed on a 6 foot table at the AMT plant. The system was subjected to some rigorous testing and it came through with *flying colors. AMT then contracted me to continuously produce bearing systems for large rotary tables. Then, instead of being a private consultant, I formed Tribos Engineering and hired employees rather than contractors. Jim Clairborne, who accompanied me here today was one of my employees. I converted my company from an S Corporation, for individuals, to a C. corporation with employees. We must have produced ten systems for AMT and the business kept coming. Then, a rather dramatic event occurred. Mr. Terwilliger took out a patent on the bearing system and put his chief engineer, Mr., Charles Goodling, as the inventor. Charles had not been involved with the bearing system development and knew very little about it. I challenged the patent and we won the case invalidating the AMT patent, and the judge disallowed any rights to AMT. That decision permitted my company to obtain a patent on the bearing systems and it opened the door to additional customers. It still remains a substantial part of our business.*

After the initial seal report was issued to NASA, I visited NASA, Glenn in Cleveland to discuss the report and suggest a follow on program. Subsequently, we received a contract to build and test prototype seals. The basic configuration is shown on the next slide. It is basically a hydrostatic configuration such that the supply air exits from both ends preventing communication between the hydrogen and oxygen. An improved version using a porous interface is shown on the next slide. Performance of the original configuration was very good, but the porous configuration had outstanding performance. Helium consumption was reduced by 80% allowing reduction in on-board helium and increased space for payload.

A presentation was made to the Stage-1 Company of Los Angeles, California, but they were not interested even though the seal would markedly improve performance of their rocket engine. We were not discouraged and converted the function of the seal from a buffer to an exclusion seal as shown on the next slide. We have received several contracts that is keeping our seal activity alive.

It was almost 10 years ago that I had thoughts about an Oil-Free engine. When I was working with Mechanical Analytics, I proposed that we consider the development of such an engine with initial concentration on the piston interface. My proposal was rejected because the company was in financial difficulty. It was not long after, that the company went bankrupt. Now some 10 years later, I am reluctant to admit how we entered the Oil-Free business, because it will be probably unbelievable to most. .The design concepts came to me in dreams. The first night a Guru appeared and told me what to do with the piston interface. The next morning, I would have our chief designer draw what the Guru described. This went on for a week or two until I had the whole engine covered from piston to crankshaft to cam shaft etc. There were many smiles from the audience and someone asked if that Guru would like a position with Major Electric. Wilson also smiled and continued. *You will note from the slides I present that hydrostatic porous carbon is being used quite extensively.* The next 6 slides presented drawings of the Oil-Free engine components, which Wilson described in detail. *As I mentioned before an external source of air pressure is required to feed all components except the piston.*

The next 4 slides described the piston compressors including their sliding air bearings that made them Oil-Free. *The demonstration engine headquartered in our plant is shown on the next slide. It is a 500 HP engine that was subjected to rigorous testing. Comparative performance is shown on the next slide. A 10 percent increase in power was achieved with a 10 percent reduction in fuel consumption. We then applied for and received some 12 patents on the technology and publicized our achievements as much as possible. We were then contacted by Major Electric to consider Oil-Free diesels for their locomotives. You all know the rest of the history as we are now heavily engaged with Major Electric and Cross Country Railroad for producing Oil-Free engines. As most of you know, our Piston compressor backup prevented a successful sabotage.*

The presentation was then interrupted by George Nation "Wilson, it is a good time to break for lunch. When we return, we would be very interested in your future plans and in your financial condition." Wilson responded, "I agree. This is a perfect spot for a break."

At lunch Wilson and Jim sat with George Nation and some other managers. There were some technical questions related to the morning presentation, but most of the conversation concerned Wilson's health. George Nation asked "Wilson, are you fully recovered from that mishap on the train?" Wilson replied, "Yes, I believe I am. My mind is clear. The presentation I am making was done solely by me, so I think that should attest to my response to your question." Nation persisted, "We believe that you ae key to any investment that Major Electric would make and we want to make sure that you are as good as ever." Wilson responded, "I can assure you George I am just as dumb now as I was before." The quip brought an immediate laugh to the entourage at the table. The food was excellent and the hour passed by quickly. Everyone returned to the meeting room at 1:00 PM and the presentation continued.

Wilson began with some organization charts. *The overall organization chart is quite simple. I am the president and Engineering reports to me. Jim Clairborne is the vice president and all administrative functions, such as marketing, human resources and accounting reports to him. The breakdown of the engineering department is shown on the next slide. The compression group is responsible for development of our piston compressors and is headed by Joshua Bentley. Most of our production is outsourced and the production group is headed by Gerry Albertelli. The design group is headed by Homer Jennings. We have an excellent technician staff headed by Robert Carpone, and finally our analysis group is headed by Julius Workman. We have an extensive library of computer codes that are used in the design process. I believe we have a very capable staff who work together to accomplish stated goals. Great things have been accomplished in a short period of time. We have a total staff of some 50 people, but it is growing every day.*

The next slide shows the revenue growth of the company. We are presently experiencing exponential growth and this year we are projecting revenue of 50 million and next year our revenue will be 70 million. As a handout we are providing our profit and loss statement as well as our balance sheet. Our net profit is about 15% of our revenue and most of the profit funds are poured back into the company. We sorely need manufacturing capability so that we can move away from the outsourcing. The next several slides describe our future plans.

Our present Oil-Free activity is limited to large engines and we need to miniaturize our components so that we can accomplish smaller engine capability with the ultimate objective of the automobile. If that becomes achievable we can become a multi-billion dollar company. Not only are there significant technical challenges, but we can expect increased competition from others that may have their own ideas that will not violate our patents. Once others grasp the simple concept of using pressurized air rather than oil we can expect many new ideas to crop up. Of course our experience and expertise puts us ahead, but we must be creative rapidly. We are working on new ideas, but I will not divulge them at this time. We are also expanding our diesel engine customer base.

With respect to our large rotary table activity, we intend to continue with our present customer base and search out other opportunities. We have managed an additional customer who uses a large rotary kiln that contains a substance that cannot communicate with oil. Our air bearing system is a natural for that application.

The piston compressors used on our Oil-Free diesel engine system can be a stand-alone product. The compressor uses the fluid being compressed as the lubricant for the sliding bearings. We anticipate a business incorporating compressors of varying sizes from small to large. We need to delve further into magnetic technology to ensure sufficient power is available for all pressure levels. Since a source of electricity is needed we have to investigate advances in battery power, including lithium-ion batteries. We are also going to consider the piston technology for liquid applications, i.e. pumps.

Our final business activity is fluid-film seals and bearings. We intend to expand applications using impregnated porous carbon. A big advantage of the porous carbon is its ability to withstand high speed rubs. Applications that come to mind include gas turbines, turbochargers, air-cycle machines and unattended air vehicles (UAV's).

Well I have filled your head with lots of material and it is time for me to sit down. We would be glad to supply you with more details at any time. I anticipate that within 5 years we will be a 100 million dollar company. We have made great strides in advancing technology that has been beneficial to the company and to mankind. Innovation is our life blood.

For your information we are considering going public with an Initial Public Offering (IPO), but we need to do significant research before a final decision is made.

Jim and I will be glad to answer any questions you may have. Thank you for your attention.

The audience gave Wilson a polite round of applause, and he took his seat.

George Nation remarked, "Wilson, we would prefer that you don't go public. We would like to be a preferred customer that might be difficult in a stockholder setting." Wilson responded, "As demonstrated by my presentation, we have ambitious plans. A primary concern is capital to support those plans and one option is to go public. However, George I can assure you that we are not acting quickly to become public. A final decision is months away."

There were a bunch of technical questions to follow. The gas turbine, jet engine and steam turbine groups were very interested in seals and bearings. The locomotive group was interested in possible upgrades. The conversations continued for at least another hour and a half.

Just before departure George Nation commented to Wilson, "Thanks for that wonderfully detailed presentation.

Listen Wilson, Please don't do anything until you hear from us." Wilson replied, "George, we are not in a hurry. Right now we are concentrating on our present commitments. We are in a growth pattern and that is consuming our energies. We believe our cash flow can sustain us without incurring additional debt. Thank you for your hospitality. I enjoyed the visit."

On the way home, Jim remarked to Wilson, "That was one hell of a presentation. I am sure something good will come of it." Wilson replied, "You know Jim, I thoroughly enjoyed conjuring up the power point presentation. It gave me a good perspective on where we have been and where we are going. It was also good for my brain and I feel I am fully recovered from the concussion." Jim replied, "Wilson, I have a feeling that you are going to have some monumental decisions to make."

Meanwhile back at Major Electric, George Nation kept his managers in the meeting room for further discussion. "Gentlemen, you have heard Wilson Shindler. I would like your opinion as to what we should do next."

Matt Shaughnessy from the locomotive group was first to speak up. "George, you know my feelings. I consider Wilson a creative genius and we should do everything in our power to bring him and his company as part of Major Electric. We would not only get a very creative guy, but also a promising enterprise." The turbine groups and jet engine divisions were very interested in the seal technology that Tribos could bring. They indicated that improvements in seal technology would significantly improve efficiency that their customers would very much like. The general consensus from all attendees was that capture of Tribos and Wilson Shindler to Major Electric would be very advantageous. They also thought that the time was ripe to do it before Tribos got too big and expensive. George Nation concluded by saying, "Thank you gentleman, for confirming my convictions. We shall immediately prepare to purchase Tribos and bring them into the Major Electric community."

DECISIONS, DECISIONS

Back at the Tribos facility, Wilson and Jim Clairborne were strategizing on how best to meet company goals. One week had elapsed since the Major Electric meeting. Jim Clairborne's cell phone rang and he answered it. "Jim this is George Nation here. How are you today?" Jim mouthed to Wilson that it was Major Electric. "I am fine George and what can I do for you today?" George replied, "Jim, we were very impressed with Wilson's presentation and we would very much like Tribos to become under the umbrella of Major Electric. We are ready to offer 60 million to obtain ownership of Tribos. There are some stipulations for this offer, such as Wilson and you guaranteeing employment for at least 5 years. Please advise Wilson's response and when we can begin negotiations." Jim responded, "George, This is more than we expected. We thought that Major Electric would invest some money in our company, but not for a full purchase. I will convey your offer to Wilson and get back to you as soon as possible." "Please do that Jim. We are quite anxious to consummate the arrangement." When Jim relayed the information to Wilson, he was quite taken aback. "I did not expect a complete take over. We have a lot of thinking to do. It wouldn't hurt to begin negotiations so that we know the terms and conditions, and we have to determine if the price is right. I think we should consult with our lawyer, Jeremy Patterson. In the meantime Jim, start laying out our conditions if we agree to be taken over. We have three possibilities, an Initial Public Offering, a takeover or to remain as we are now. We have to list advantages and disadvantages of each before a decision can be made." Jim replied, "We will start immediately. You will have to admit Wilson, it is a nice dilemma to have."

That evening, Wilson told Maureen of the situation. "We have three options. 1) Going public, 2) Being bought out by Major Electric or 3) Remaining as we are now." Maureen replied, "Wilson let me tell you something. You cannot continue to work 12 to 14 hours a day 7 days a week. A slowdown is necessary or else you will become a premature corpse and a decision will not matter. Please, in consideration of your wife and son, make a decision that will bring you back to a normal life." Wilson had no reply, but the message was clear and ingrained in his brain. He realized that he had been neglecting his family, and inwardly he felt ashamed. The phone rang and Maureen answered it. "Hello, Mrs. Shindler. This is Stanislaus Neeley and I am calling to inquire about Wilson's health. Has he recovered from the concussion?" Maureen replied, "Yes, he is doing quite well, but I will let him tell you himself, and thank you for asking." Maureen told

Wilson who it was and she gave him the phone. "Hello Stanislaus, it is good of you to call. We have been using the C-5 resin quite extensively. I think we should start paying for it. My doctors tell me that I have recovered from the concussion and I can return to my old schedule, but I have chosen to slow down somewhat. " Stanislaus replied, "Don't concern yourself about the resin. It is my pleasure to accommodate Tribos." Wilson commented, "Stanislaus, I could use your advice on some business matters that have arisen. Is there a chance we could get together and talk?" Stanislaus replied, "I would love to meet you and chat. I think that we should have done it long before. Why don't you and Maureen come to our house this weekend for dinner and we could mix business with pleasure? My wife Beatrice would love to chat with Maureen. We generally eat at 6, so why don't you come about 5:00 PM or so?" Wilson interjected, "That's very kind of you. I have been wanting to meet with you for some time. We will be at your home around 5:00 PM." Maureen was elated and very much looking forward to meeting with the wealthy set.

The Neeley home was some 10 miles away from the Shindler home. It was located in the elite section of town where a group of mansions were situated. Neeley's property was surrounded by a large fence and guards were stationed at the entrance gates. Wilson was directed to a parking location and he and Maureen walked to the front entrance. The home was a huge brick structure adorned with several large bay windows and all other windows were decorated with large ornate shutters. A small well-manicured garden was displayed at the side of the entrance walk and the doorway area was protected with an attractive roofed structure. Wilson rang the doorbell and chimes rang out inside. A maid servant answered the door and behind her stood Stanislaus and Beatrice.

Stanislaus was a tall man with silver wavy hair. There seemed to be no fat on his body and he was in remarkable shape for an octogenarian. His face had sharp features and his blue eyes tinkled with expression. Beatrice too was in great shape for her age with a thin tall body. No doubt they were a handsome couple and they seemed to be enjoying their elder years. Stanislaus interjected, "We finally meet. Please come in. Marie will take your coats." The two woman were anxious to talk with one another and they glided towards each other. Maureen commented, "You have a beautiful home and the grounds are marvelous." Beatrice replied, "It is much too big for the two of us. We keep it to satisfy our children, grandchildren and great grandchildren. We are seriously thinking of selling it and moving to senior quarters

211

somewhere. However, I am not sure we don't have a white elephant here. It would not be easy to sell this place." The mention of children aroused Maureen and the two women retired to a sitting room to continue their chat.

The men went into a den type room adjacent to the living room. Stanislaus began the conversation, "I am interested in knowing what I could possibly be giving you advice about. I have read of your great success with an Oil-Free engine and that in a 10 year span you have made wonderful advancement with your company." Wilson replied, "Stanislaus, I am in a dilemma as to what to do next. There are three possibilities. We could go public, we could be bought out by Major Electric, or we could just maintain the status quo. Perhaps you had to face a similar decision in the past. I thought that you might be able to shed some light on the situation and direct me on an appropriate path." Stanislaus replied, "Whoa, that's quite a dilemma to be in. I had no such choice. We just worked our tails off as a private company. Raising capital was not so easy. We did it through bank loans, but interest rates were quite high and there were many a time that we thought we might default. What saved us was the development of the C-5 resin that we supply to you. The demand for that product sky rocketed and provided the funds to pay our loans, produce expansion facilities and still make a good profit. We then were able to develop new products and continue our expansion. However, we still have a considerable debt load to pay off, and the way capitalism works, we will never be free of debt and I am sure it will be necessary to go to the bank well again for additional capital. Going public was not an option with me as I was too dictatorial to give up control to a stranger board of directors and stock holders who knew nothing about our operations. However, once I retired, the operation passed on to another family member and that doesn't always work out for the best, witness my son Horace. I would not be so audacious as to advise you what path to take. I can only suggest that you decide, what you want to accomplish and select the path that best gets you there. I would also suggest that you alone make the decision. Do not listen to the 'so called experts', and follow your heart as well as your brain and you will come to the right decision." Wilson listened intently to what Stanislaus had to say, and he especially liked the part that indicated that he alone would make the decision and not to listen to advice from others.

Marie interjected and announced to Stanislaus and Wilson that dinner was being served. When the two men entered the dining room Beatrice and Maureen were already seated. Maureen exclaimed, "Beatrice and I had a wonderful conversation. The Neeley's had three children, two girls and a boy." Maureen knew quite a bit of the Neeley family history in the short conversation she had with Beatrice and vice versa, Beatrice found out lots of information about the Shindler family history. The two woman liked each other immediately as did the two men. Prior to the meeting Stanislaus and Wilson admired the exploits of each other and a bonded family friendship was formed in a very short time. The prime rib meal was excellent, and before the visit ended, dates were set for future meetings.

The next day at the Tribos plant, Wilson called Jim Clairborne into his office and proclaimed, "I want to come to a decision within the next couple of days. Let's go through the plus and minus exercise of each possibility." Jim answered, "Yes, let's do that. I am being pressured by both Julius Bergdoff and George Nation to come to a decision." Wilson replied, "We are not going to be rushed into an IPO or a takeover. I want a thorough understanding of what we will get into so that a clear decision will be possible. Have you had any time to consider advantages and disadvantages?" Jim replied, "Yes I have, but it needs more work and I would like a couple of days of uninterrupted time." Wilson agreed, "Yes, let's meet again in three days and we must refuse calls from both Bergdoff and Nation. We should tell them that their offers are under consideration and a decision will be forthcoming in a few days. In the interim, I too will investigate the consequences of both opportunities. We must also keep in mind that we can also continue without accepting either offer."

Three days later the two men met again. Jim began, "I have spent the last two days, full time and then some, researching our options. I will try to summarize and avoid minutia. Let's start with an IPO. A distinct advantage of going public is that the money received does not require payback. It is there to use as working capital, debt depletion. merger and acquisitions, etc. Also, once you have a public stock company, additional shares can be issued to increase capital. Many companies go public and raise a considerable amount of capital. There are also many disadvantages. An IPO itself is not a cheap proposition. There are considerable amounts of legal and accounting fees. The Board of Directors must be made up of prominent personages who will not be cheap. There are many government regulations to contend with and it would be necessary to hire a dedicated staff to provide regulatory information. It would be difficult to maintain proprietary information secret. The company would become an open book. Every quarter would have to be better than the previous one to maintain a high stock price. An unfriendly takeover is possible through share buyout. Also, activists shareholders may exist who would want to take over the company and replace personnel. As CEO you would be encumbered with administrative details that would take you away from your technical and engineering activities. I could get into more details if you so desire." Wilson responded, "No need to do that. Your summaries are fine." Clairborne continued, "O.K. Let's discuss a Major Electric takeover. Incidentally, for your information they have upped the bid to 70 million. The advantages are as follows: You have the resources of a major organization at your back. For example, production facilities, which we do not have. There are multiple opportunities for increased business internally. For example, seal business for their rotating machines, and of course our ongoing locomotive diesel engine business. They could be very helpful in expanding our piston compressor business. The downside is that they own the business and could do with it what they may. It is likely that they would want us to proceed as we are doing, but there is always the chance they might throw in the towel. I will say this, negotiations have gone very well and they are quite anxious to have us on board. I believe that we could have a very productive relationship.

The third option is to remain as we are. The primary advantage is that you remain in control and you basically own the organization. That could possibly mean that you could become a billionaire down the road. The disadvantages are that our debt would increase because of continuous bank borrowings and progress would be on a slow path. For example, we would have to build a production facility from scratch and that would take considerable time. I think that from these summaries, you have a pretty good idea of the option characteristics. The ball is now in your court to come to a decision. "Wilson responded, "I will make a decision shortly."

That evening, Wilson called Stanislaus. After Wilson's conversation, Stanislaus replied, "I see that you not only followed your head, but also your heart. Good luck, I only wish you the best. More importantly, when can we get together again? Beatrice had a wonderful time with Maureen and she wants to see her again and I enjoyed talking to you immensely." Wilson replied, "Well it is our turn to be the host. How about this weekend?" Stanislaus interjected, "You know Wilson, at our age travel is a chore. We much rather that you visit us here. We have all the help we need and we can spend all our time conversing. How about Saturday at 5:00 PM?" Wilson concluded, "O.K. Stanislaus, it will be nice to see you again."

EMPLOYEE PRESENTATION

Several days later, Wilson asked Jim Clairborne to arrange an employee wide meeting in the large workspace where the demo diesel was located. I will need microphone facilities and a screen and projector for a power point presentation. Jim inquired, "Wilson, have you made your decision?" Wilson responded, "Yes, I have. You and everyone else will find out at the meeting. I think it would be advisable to have local press coverage." Jim responded, "I will see to it Wilson."

The meeting was arranged to occur several days later. All employees were present, and the local press attended in force. A projector and large screen was installed. Promptly at 2:00 PM Wilson entered and walked to the podium.

Good afternoon ladies and gentlemen. Over the past ten years our company has made great technological advances. Today we are busy supplying Oil-Free locomotive engines, large rotary table bearing systems and exclusion seals, among other things. We have aroused significant interest in the corporate world that has led to some important opportunities. We have been approached by a well-known underwriter, to become a public company. We have also been approached by a large company, namely Major Electric as a buyout. As a third option we can consider staying as we are. Since I am the majority stockholder of this company, my decision determines what we will do. For the past several days, I have considered these options very carefully. I was told by a very wise man that I should not only go with my brains, but also with my heart. My ultimate objective, with respect to our company, is new technology. I cannot describe the feeling of satisfaction that I get when advanced technology, such as the Oil-Free diesel or the large rotary table gas bearings, are successful. With that objective in mind, what option will provide the greatest opportunity for new technology development? The answer to me was obvious. We are going to become part of the Major Electric family. They have tremendous resources, such as manufacturing that will be available to us. Every employee will be given compatible salarys with improved fringe benefits. We are in the process of negotiations, which should be concluded in approximately two months. The takeover does not mean that we do not have to make a profit. We still have to contribute to the parent organization. That can be done not only through an outside customer base, but to internal assistance as well. Several hours ago I spoke to George Nation, the CEO of Major Electric and he was thrilled with the decision and promised complete cooperation with our requirements. I have assigned Jim Clairborne as our chief negotiator and he will report to me as progress develops. I *feel very comfortable with the decision and I believe that every one of you will benefit from the merger.*

Now I would like to change the conversation to our future endeavors and I will present slide information on our business plan, which was previously presented to Major Electric.

Our present Oil-Free activity is limited to large engines and we need to miniaturize our components so that we can accomplish smaller engine capability with the ultimate objective of the automobile. If that becomes achievable we can become a multi-billion dollar company. Not only are there significant technical challenges, but we can expect increased competition from others that may have their own ideas that will not violate our patents. Once others grasp the simple concept of using pressurized air rather than oil we can expect many new ideas to crop up. Of course our experience and expertise puts us ahead, but we must be continuously creative.

With respect to our large rotary table activity, we intend to continue with our present customer base and search out other opportunities. We have managed an additional customer who uses a large rotary kiln that contains a substance that cannot communicate with oil. Our air bearing system is a natural for that application.

The piston compressors used on our Oil-Free diesel engine system can be a stand-alone product. The compressor uses the fluid being compressed as the lubricant for the sliding bearings. We anticipate a business incorporating compressors of varying sizes from small to large. We need to delve further into magnetic technology to ensure sufficient power is available for all pressure levels. Since a source of electricity is needed we have to investigate advances in battery power, including lithium-ion batteries. We are also going to consider the piston technology for liquid applications, i.e. pumps.

Our final business activity is fluid-film seals and bearings. We intend to expand applications using impregnated porous carbon. A big advantage of the porous carbon is its ability to withstand high speed rubs. Applications that come to mind include gas turbines, turbochargers, air-cycle machines and unattended air vehicles (UAV's).

There is no doubt in my mind, that our success is due to our personnel. I anticipate that within 5 years we will be a 100 million dollar organization. We have made great strides in advancing technology that has been beneficial to the company and to mankind. Innovation is our life blood.

I want to thank you for your hard work, inventiveness, cooperation with each other and I look forward to your continued contributions as we enter a new phase and become a part of the Major Electric organization.

According to the terms of the agreement, Wilson was required to commit at least 5 years to Major Electric.

A NEW LIFE

On Saturday evening Wilson and Maureen were again visiting with Stanislaus and Bernice. New social relationships had developed for both couples as they enjoyed each other's company immensely. Wilson explained his reasoning for the Major Electric decision to Stanislaus and the progress of the negotiations. Maureen discussed her son's progress as an oncologist in Boston. They all discussed current events and the political environment. Both couples had like beliefs so the discussions were very civil and enjoyable. As Wilson left for the evening he felt that a new page had occurred in his life. He would become more socially active and a better family man. The feeling was good and he looked forward to the future.

Prior to final negotiations, it occurred to Wilson that he was about to become a mutli-millionaire. Since he owned practically all of the stock of Tribos, a buyout meant he would cede his shares to Major Electric for the buying price of 70 million dollars. He discussed the situation with Maureen. "I don't know all our options or what's the best way to proceed. I do know that I must share some proceeds with my staff who has helped us get where we are. I also want to contribute to our son's research at the hospital to accelerate his success, and I think we should consider philanthropy." Maureen replied.

"This is very exciting Wilson. I would love to be involved. I have always wanted to assist the unfortunate, but never had the resources to do it on a grand scale." Wilson responded, "Good, I will see that you have a major role."

The following day, Wilson called his lawyer, Jeremy Patterson. "Jeremy, my company, Tribos Engineering is being bought out by Major Electric. I want to redistribute shares of stock and also form a charitable organization. When can we get together?" That afternoon, the two men huddled in Patterson's office. The final breakdown was as follows:

Wilson Shindler, private accumulation, 20 million dollars

Selected Tribos personnel, Jim Clairborne, Homer Jennings, Bob Carpone and department heads, 15 million dollars.

Charitable organization – 35 million dollars.

Several months later, all the smoke had cleared and operations were on an even keel. Under Maureen's leadership, things were going well with the charitable organization. Her concentration was on the homeless. Working with other organizations, she was able to increase living quarters by 20%. Her finances were stable due to investments and outside contributions.

Wilson was quite happy at work and relations with Major Electric were very smooth. Progress and advancements had been made on Oil-Free technology for smaller engines. Also, significant progress was made on seal technology that other divisions of Major Electric were using.

Wilson finished breakfast at home, kissed his wife on her cheek, and exclaimed, "Some ten years ago I kissed you goodbye as I left for Mechanical Analytics to persuade them to invest in an Oil- Free engine. A lot of water has passed over the dam since then. We have a new life now, and I must say, I like it, I like it."

THE END

BIOGRAPHY

Wilbur Shapiro is retired from an engineering career that had spanned over 50 years. He has produced over 58 publications in the technical literature and 10 patents. He has always had a penchant for writing and Oil-Free is his third publication. He has made writing at an advanced age a second career. Mr. Shapiro resides in Albany, NY with Muriel his wife of 56 years.

Publications of Wilbur Shapiro

(1) Anecdotal Odes of Wilbur Shapiro

(2) Fore

(3) Oil-Free

Made in the USA
Middletown, DE
20 February 2015